I0668010

The Pilgrim's Progress

by

James Martin Charlton

Adapted from the book by
John Bunyan

TSL Publications

First published in Great Britain in 2024
By TSL Publications, Rickmansworth

Copyright © 2024 James Martin Charlton.

ISBN: 978-1-915660-94-7

The right of James Martin Charlton. to be identified as the author of this work
has been asserted by the author in accordance with the UK Copyright, Designs
and Patents Act 1988.

All characters and events in this publication, other than those clearly in the
public domain, are fictitious and any resemblance to actual persons, living or
dead, is purely coincidental.

All rights reserved. No part of this publication may be reproduced, stored in a
retrieval system or transmitted, in any form or by any means without the prior
written permission of the publisher, nor be otherwise circulated in any form of
binding or cover other than that in which it is published and without a similar
condition being imposed on the subsequent buyer.

Cover design

Phillip Block

Adapting *The Pilgrim's Progress* for the Stage

In adapting Bunyan's *The Pilgrim's Progress* for the stage, I discovered that the work contains many striking parallels with works of English drama from both before his time and after.

In 2000, I was commissioned by the Royal Shakespeare Company to adapt John Bunyan's novel *The Pilgrim's Progress* for the stage. I had pitched the RSC a number of projects and this was the one the then Literary Manager, Simon Reade, went for. I had wanted to adapt the book for some time. I had been developing an idiosyncratic form of drama based on Christian tropes and imagery, beginning with my award-winning play *Fat Souls* (performed at the Warehouse Theatre, Croydon in 1993). These plays used ancient theatrical devices such as direct speech to the audience, masks, verse and metaphoric language, and emblematic characters. These plays were intended to stages stories which were written like the scroll in *Revelation* 5:1, in some translations referred to as being "written within and without." They are plays which might be set in the world, or in a psyche. I felt that Bunyan's great allegory had this quality, and I approached it as such.

Despite it being one of the great classics of English literature and one of the biggest selling books of all time, stage adaptations of *The Pilgrim's Progress* had been few and far between. The only major stage production I am aware of being performed in my lifetime was by the Prospect Theatre Company, on tour and at the Old Vic in 1974/5. I can recall seeing a large photograph from it displayed in the foyer of the Old Vic in the early 1980s, I believe showing Christian facing down Apollyon. I read somewhere that Carl Davies scored it almost as a musical but know little else about it. Perhaps the fact that *Pilgrim* hasn't been adapted many times, unlike *The Canterbury Tales* or *Robinson Crusoe*, meant that it was not suited for theatre adaptation? Yet the bulk of Bunyan's allegory is written in dialogue and the characters have a vitality which makes them innately theatrical.

The book was written a decade or so after the Restoration of the Monarchy in 1660 and the lifting of the Puritan ban on theatre performances. Bunyan's characterisation is at times not dissimilar to that found in the Restoration playwrights – there is a linkage between Bunyan's Mr Worldly Wiseman and By-Ends and Etheridge's Sir Fopling Flutter in *The Man of Mode*. Bunyan's larger-than-life characters are made to explode onto the stage. These roles are made for the kinds of fruity, refined acting that was still rife in the RSC at the turn of the millennium. Bunyan's words cry out to be spoken and savoured by classically trained voices. Actors habituated to Shakespeare's language would relish such lines as Wiseman's "Beshrew him for his counsel!" or The Man in the Iron Cage's "I have so hardened my heart I cannot repent." A great deal of my work consisted of redacting a book of over 100,000 words to a manageable stage length whilst preserving as much of Bunyan's idiom as possible.

Whilst Bunyan's language and characterisation has much in common with that found in the Jacobean and Caroline stage writers, his sense of drama and action has analogues in much earlier English stage works. His characters' actions fit with a rigid adherence to the values attached to their name, akin to the medieval Morality plays. Some of the action is strikingly similar. In the old play of *The Summoning of Everyman*, the title character (a close cousin of *Pilgrim's* Christian) scourges himself in penance for his sins after meeting a character called Confession. In *The Pilgrim's Progress*, Christian and his companion Hopeful are scourged by a Shining One for the sin of falling for the wiles of The Flatterer. Everyman and Christian's stories end very similarly, as both of them cross the border between life and death and both end up in heaven (which in Bunyan is called "the Celestial City"), both being met by Angels. It is as if Bunyan was using the dramaturgy of the Medieval stage to shape his action.

At the time I was commissioned by the RSC to adapt *The Pilgrim's Progress*, they were staging a rare revival of G Bernard Shaw's 1921 play cycle *Back to Methuselah*. I saw this in Stratford's The Other Place theatre in late 2000. The experience of watching this enormous, verbose but wildly stimulating work gave me a great deal of inspiration for my adaptation. Shaw wrote about his affinity with Bunyan on a number of occasions, and even professed to prefer him to Shakespeare – "All that you miss in Shakespear [sic] you find in Bunyan" he declares in an 1897 review of a production of *King Lear* (reprinted in *Our Theatre in the Nineties*). As my version of *Pilgrim* began to take shape on the page, it began to resemble the text of a Shaw play, with eccentric characters engaged in long, passionate arias expounding their views and attempting to convince others of their positions. Bunyan, like Shaw, can be very funny, and there is much enjoyment to be had from watching the squirming of By Ends and the self-aggrandisement of Ignorance.

More contemporary dramatic similarities helped me adapt the scene in Doubting Castle to the stage. Whereas I bring Apollyon on stage and he engages Christian in a bout of stage combat, I didn't want to introduce Gant

Despair as a pantomime giant into this latter, deeply moving chapter of the story. Christian and Hopeful become trapped by their own existential despair and cannot move from the giant's clutches. I begin this scene with an echo of Samuel Beckett's masterpiece of existential stasis *Waiting for Godot*, as Christian announces that there's "nothing to be done" in terms of escaping. The scene progresses with the Giant present as a huge, gloomy shadow cast over the men. The two pilgrims lay on the floor of the dungeon, bemoaning their fate and no longer even communicating with each other – they are lost in their own desperate monologues. After Beckett, the scene draws on Sarah Kane's final play, *4:48 Psychosis*, to show that the characters are trapped in their own mental crises. Of course, in Kane's plays the characters (like their author) never escape from despair; Bunyan's characters do find a way out of desperation and unlock the door into a positive, active attitude to life. This is one of the reasons I wanted to adapt him, as an alternative to the sense of doubt and hopelessness which pervaded much of the stage writing in the UK at the turn of the millennium.

The version I delivered to the RSC was an enormous piece. I wrote it for a large, publicly funded company and, even with doubling, it would require at least 16 actors to perform. Very soon after I delivered the piece, Simon Reade (who'd commissioned the play) left his position and the adaptation never found another supporter within the RSC. Few professional theatre companies in the UK can afford something as resource-heavy as my play turned out to be, and it has yet to find an alternative home. Perhaps one day an amateur or community theatre group might take it up.

Bunyan, I discovered through writing my adaptation of *The Pilgrim's Progress*, is one of the best playwrights that the British theatre never had. My adaptation bears elements of the Elizabethan and Restoration drama, Jacobean comedies and masques, Shavian political drama, the theatre of the absurd, and contemporary psychological expressionism. Bunyan deserves his place on the stage, as the English stage is already well versed in the essentials of Bunyan.

A version of this introduction appeared in the Spring 2015 issue of
The Recorder, the newsletter of the International Bunyan Society.

The Pilgrim's Progress
by John Bunyan, adapted for the stage
by James Martin Charlton

The following is a breakdown of the scenes in the play, also listing characters by the scene in which they first appear.

PART ONE

1. Invocation of the Dream
THE DREAMER
THE DREAMING LADY

2. Leaving Home
CHRISTIAN, a pilgrim
CHRISTIANA, his wife
SON
DAUGHTER

EVANGELIST

OBSTINATE
PLIABLE

HELP

3. Mr Worldly Wiseman
MR WORLDLY WISEMAN
MOSES

GOOD WILL

4. The House of the Interpreter
THE INTERPRETER

OLD MAN, a sweeper
MAID, a cleaner
STOUT MAN
MAN IN AN IRON CAGE
MAN IN BED, who dreams of the last judgement

THREE SHINING ONES

5. The Lesson at the Arbour
SIMPLE
SLOTH
PRESUMPTION

ANOTHER PILGRIM

MISTRUST
TIMOROUS

6. House Beautiful
PORTER

PIETY
PRUDENCE
CHARITY

7. Two Valleys
APOLLYON, a monster

DEMONS
HOBGOBLIN

8. Christian, Faithful & Talkative
FAITHFUL

TALKATIVE

9. Mercy & Evangelist's Prophecy
MERCY

PART TWO

10. Vanity Fair
BARKER
TRADERS
ROGUE
FOOL
KNAVE
BAWD
DRAB
GREAT ONE, of the Fair
GENT
GAOLER

11. The trial of Faithful
USHER
LORD HATEGOOD, the judge

Witnesses
ENVY
SUPERSTITION
PICKTHANK

The Jury
MR BLINDMAN
MRS NO-GOOD
MR MALICE
MR LOVE-LUST
MRS LIVE-LOOSE
MR HEADY
MR HIGH-MIND
MR ENMITY
MR LIAR
MRS CRUELTY
MR HATE-LIGHT
MR IMPLACABLE

HOPEFUL, another pilgrim

12. By-Ends
BY-ENDS
MR HOLD-THE-WORLD
MR MONEY-LOVE
MR SAVE-ALL

13. Giant Despair

14. The Shepherds of the Delectable Mountains
KNOWLEDGE
EXPERIENCE
WATCHFUL
SINCERE

Suggestions for Doubling

Actor 1
Dreamer / Christian

Actor 2
Dreaming Lady / Christiana / Mrs No-Good

Actor 3
Evangelist / The Interpreter / Porter / Mr Hate-Light / Knowledge / The Flatterer / The King

Actor 4
Obstinate / Man in the Iron Cage / Mistrust / Great One / Envy / Mr Enmity / Mr Money-Love / 1st Shining One after River

Actor 5
Pliable / Man in Bed / Timorous / Fool / Superstition / Mr Liar / Mr Save-All / 2nd Shining One after River

Actor 6
Mr Worldly Wiseman / Apollyon / Lord Hategood / Mr Hold-the-World / Atheist

Actor 7
Son / Knave / Mr Love-Lust

Actor 8
Daughter / Drab / Miss Live-Loose

Actor 9
Moses / Old Man / 1st Shining One after Interpreter's House / Presumption / Gaoler / Mr Malice / Experience

Actor 10
Help / Stout Man / 2nd Shining One after Interpreter's House / Sloth / Gent / Mr Heady / Watchful

Actor 11
Good Will / Charity / Mercy / Mrs Cruelty / Sincere

Actor 12
Maid / 3rd Shining One after Interpreter's House / Simple / Piety /
Bawd / Madam High-Mind

Actor 13
Another Pilgrim / Faithful / Hopeful

Actor 14
Prudence / Talkative / Barker / Pickthank / Mr Blindman / By-Ends

Actor 15
Hobgoblin / Rogue / Usher / Mr Implacable / Ignorance

Part One

1

INVOCATION OF THE DREAM

(*A bed. A man,* DREAMER, *a product of 500 years of Protestant culture – is about to get into bed and dream his old dream. His other half,* DREAMING LADY, *listens beside him.*)

DREAMER: As I walk through the wilderness of this world.

LADY: You think our world is a wilderness?

DREAMER: I light on a certain place, where there is a Denn.

LADY: Are you not happy here?

DREAMER: And I lay me down in this place to sleep.

LADY: Your heart's not in us.

DREAMER: And as I sleep I dream a dream.

LADY: I sleep beside thee. Together we dream.

(*They get into bed.*)

DREAMER: Dreams of being alone.

LADY: Dreams of being apart.

DREAMER: Dreams of separation.

LADY: Dreams of suffering.

DREAMER: Dreams of achieving that connection none can ever break.

LADY: Nightmare that my dream is crossing yours.

(*The* DREAMER *turns to face his* LADY.)

DREAMER: Do you know what? Last night I had the oddest dream.

LADY: I suppose you have to tell me.

DREAMER: I listen to your dreams.

LADY: Do you?

DREAMER: All the time.

LADY: Go on.

DREAMER: I dreamed I was a man.

LADY: Dream on.

DREAMER: This ain't to be mocked at!

LADY: I said go on.

(*As The* DREAMER *tells us of his dream, he changes into the person he is describing.*)

DREAMER: I dreamed that I am clothed with rags and a book is in my hand.

LADY: Which book?

DREAMER: The Bible.

LADY: Here we go.

DREAMER: And on my back is a great burden. I open the book and read therein...

(*He opens the book and reads; as he reads he weeps and trembles.*)

(*In the dream*) O What shall I do?!

LADY: You were alone in this dream?

DREAMER: I had a wife and two small children.

(*Two children, a* SON *and a* DAUGHTER, *appear on the periphery.*)

SON: Dad!

DAUGHTER: Daddy!

LADY: This family of yours, you love them?

DREAMER: My burden is very heavy.

LADY: This wife: what does she look like?

DREAMER: You.

LADY: You better tell me everything.

DREAMER: I will.

(*The scene changes and the bedroom becomes a kitchen. The* LADY *becomes* CHRISTIANA, CHRISTIAN's *wife. The* CHILDREN *rush to the kitchen table which* CHRISTIANA *is laying. They grab at bread and the* LADY *smacks their hands away. The* DREAMER *staggers under the weight of his burden. They sit at the table, now lost in the dream.*)

*

2
LEAVING HOME

(CHRISTIAN, *suffering under the weight of his burden, is at the kitchen table with his wife* CHRISTIANA *and their* SON *and* DAUGHTER. *The* CHILDREN *impatiently bang their cutlery.* CHRISTIAN *shrinks from them.* CHRISTIANA *notices this but ignores it, placing a bowl of eggs on the table which the* CHILDREN *grab and tuck greedily into.* CHRISTIANA *begins cutting some bread when her husband cries out.*)

CHRISTIAN: O my dear Wife, and you the children of my bowels!

CHRISTIANA: Here we go.

(*The* CHILDREN *eye their parents nervously.*)

CHRISTIAN: I your dear friend am in myself undone, by reason of this burden lies hard upon me.

(CHRISTIANA *sighs.*)

Our city will be burned with fire from heaven, and we shall all miserably come to ruin except we find some way of escape.

(*Pause.*)

CHRISTIANA: Some frenzy distemper has got in your brain.

(*The* SON *giggles. The* DAUGHTER *whimpers, scared.* CHRISTIANA *turns on them.*)

Go to your room.

SON: But Mother...

CHRISTIANA: Go to your room!

(*The* CHILDREN *rush out.* CHRISTIANA *turns to* CHRISTIAN.)

I can't stand this for very much longer.

CHRISTIAN: Each day the pain is worsened.

CHRISTIANA: Is that any wonder? Always buried in that book.

CHRISTIAN: This book's the only thing makes any sense to me.

CHRISTIANA: The only thing?

(CHRISTIAN *nods*.)

Husband, I have tried. But I cannot see owt but self-indulgence in this your strangeness.

CHRISTIAN: If you knew what pain I suffer!

CHRISTIANA: If you knew how much this conduct pains me and my brood! Do you ever think of us?

CHRISTIAN: I can think of nothing but enclosure tight in suffering's nutshell.

CHRISTIANA: My heart once was open and soft to you. Within my breast I feel it hardening. Wait. It is closed.

(CHRISTIANA *goes for* CHRISTIAN.)

Be a man, sir. Desists these antics! We'll speak again when your manners mend.

CHRISTIAN: I shall pray for you.

CHRISTIANA: Much good that will do!

(*Exit* CHRISTIANA.

CHRISTIAN *spends a sleepless night of sighs and tears.*

A dull morning rises. Enter CHRISTIANA *and the* CHILDREN.)

CHRISTIANA: How do you this morning?

CHRISTIAN: Worse and worse.

(*The* DAUGHTER *bursts into tears*.)

SON: Shh!

CHRISTIANA: (*To the* CHILDREN.) Come on, lessons.

DAUGHTER: What's the matter with Daddy?

SON: Father's bedlam bound.

CHRISTIANA: I said lessons!

          (CHRISTIANA *shoos them on their way and* CHRISTIAN *is left alone.*)

CHRISTIAN: A stranger in a strange land.

          (CHRISTIAN *rises and the kitchen becomes a field.*)

          What shall I do to be saved?!

          (CHRISTIAN *sobs. A man,* EVANGELIST, *approaches* CHRISTIAN.)

EVANGELIST: Why do you cry?

          (CHRISTIAN *almost jumps out of his skin, then calms.*)

CHRISTIAN: Sir, I perceive by this book I am condemned to die and after that come to Judgement. The first I'm not able to do, nor am I willing to do the second.

EVANGELIST: Why not willing to die?

CHRISTIAN: Lower than the grave this burden on my back will sink me!

EVANGELIST: Why standeth thee so still?

          (EVANGELIST *produces a parchment roll which he unfurls before* CHRISTIAN. EVANGELIST *reads out loud what's written on it.*)

          FLY THE COMING WRATH!

CHRISTIAN: Wither?

          (EVANGELIST *points with his finger.*)

EVANGELIST: See yonder Little Gate?

CHRISTIAN: No.

EVANGELIST: See yonder shining light?

CHRISTIAN: Think so.

EVANGELIST: Keep that light in your eye, go there directly. Soon thou shalt see the Gate. Go to it and knock. There it shall be told thee what to do. Why wait you? Run.

CHRISTIAN: Run?

EVANGELIST: For your ETERNAL LIFE!

CHRISTIAN: Run for my LIFE ETERNAL!

(CHRISTIAN *begins to run, free as the wind.*)

(*Repeating.*) Run run run run for my Eternal Life!

(CHRISTIANA *appears and watches him leg it.*)

CHRISTIANA: Hold on!

CHRISTIAN: Run for my LIFE ETERNAL!!!

(*The* DREAMING LADY *becomes the forlorn* CHRISTIANA, *some way behind, watching her husband go.*)

CHRISTIANA: Where do you think you're going? Husband get back here! What about your poor family?

(*The* CHILDREN *appear.*)

SON: Where speeds father?

DAUGHTER: Daddy? Daddy?!

CHRISTIANA: It appears your father's left us my dears.

(CHRISTIANA *and the* CHILDREN *look broken-heartedly after their father. Two neighbours –* OBSTINATE *and* PLIABLE *– enter to them.*)

OBSTINATE: Awful news has reached our ears.

PLIABLE: How fast doth he leg it!

CHRISTIANA: O my good neighbours! My husband's out of his wits.

OBSTINATE: We shall drag him back – if necessary, by force.

PLIABLE: You think we ought?

OBSTINATE: Move it!

CHRISTIANA: Tell him we need him despite all!

(OBSTINATE *and* PLIABLE *begin to run after* CHRISTIAN. CHRISTIANA *hugs her* CHILDREN *to her and recedes into the background.* CHRISTIAN *is running out of the town.*)

CHRISTIAN: Life! Life! Eternal Life!
Life! Life! Eternal Life!
Life! Life! Eternal...

(OBSTINATE *and* PLIABLE *catch up with* CHRISTIAN *and stand in his way.*)

OBSTINATE: Halt!

CHRISTIAN: Neighbours, wherefore do you appear?

OBSTINATE: Come back with us.

CHRISTIAN: By no means. You dwell in the city of Destruction where I was born. I see it so now. Sooner or later dying there, you will sink into a place of fire and brimstone. Neighbours, come with me.

OBSTINATE: I should say so! Leave our friends and comforts behind us?

CHRISTIAN: All you forsake is not to be compared with a little of that I seek.

OBSTINATE: What do you seek since you leave all the world to find it?

CHRISTIAN: An inheritance that does not fade. Read if you will in my book.

OBSTINATE: Tush! Away with your book. Come back!

CHRISTIAN: My hand's to the plough.

OBSTINATE: There's a company of these craze-headed coxcombs when they take a fancy are wiser than seven men in their own eyes. Let's home, good neighbour Pliable.

PLIABLE: Don't revile. If what good Christian says is true, the things he looks for are better than ours. My heart inclines to go with him.

OBSTINATE: More fools still! Who knows where a brain-sick fellow will lead you. Be ruled by me.

CHRISTIAN: Come with me good Pliable. There are such things as I speak of and many more glories besides.

PLIABLE: Neighbour Obstinate, I intend to cast in my lot with him.

                (*To* CHRISTIAN.) But good companion you do know the way to the place?

CHRISTIAN: I got directions from Evangelist.

PLIABLE: Let's go!

OBSTINATE: Misled fantastical fellows.

                (*Exit* OBSTINATE. PLIABLE *and* CHRISTIAN *turn to each other. They giggle excitedly and shake hands. They begin walking across the plain.*)

CHRISTIAN: I'm glad you're persuaded to come along with me.

PLIABLE: Tell me further what things – and how to be enjoyed – where we travel.

CHRISTIAN: An endless kingdom and everlasting life that we may forever live therein.

PLIABLE: What else?

CHRISTIAN: Crowns of glory given us, and garments to make us shine sun-like.

PLIABLE: What else?

CHRISTIAN: No more sorrow. He that's owner of the place banishes all tears.

PLIABLE: What company shall we keep?

CHRISTIAN: Seraphim and cherubim will dazzle thine eyes. Also you'll meet thousands have gone before us. Holy and loving. Holy virgins with golden harps...

PLIABLE: This is enough to ravish one's heart! How shall we get there?

CHRISTIAN: If we're truly willing, the Lord shall bestow all on us for free.

PLIABLE: Let us mend our pace.

CHRISTIAN: Because of my burden I cannot go that fast.

(*The two of them fall into a miry slough.*
CHRISTIAN *begins to sink in the mire.*)

PLIABLE: Good neighbour Christian, where are we now?

CHRISTIAN: I know not.

PLIABLE: A fine mess you've gotten us in! Is this the joy you promised? If we have such ills at our setting out, what might we expect anon? Enjoy Heaven on your own!

(*With that,* PLIABLE *gives a desperate struggle and gets out of the mire. He goes back home.*
CHRISTIAN *wallows in the slough alone.*)

CHRISTIAN: How could such a one as me think to get Eternal Life?
Lusts and inward corruptions drag me down.
My soul is clogged with guilt.
I drown in conviction of sin.
I am scum and filth.
Help!!! Help!!!

(*A man,* HELP, *is passing near the slough.*)

HELP: That's my name, don't wear it out. What you doing?

CHRISTIAN: I fell in.

HELP: Didn't you look for the steps? Gimme your hand.

(CHRISTIAN *takes* HELP's *hand.* HELP *draws him out of the mire.*)

Right horrible old place that, ain't it? They call it "the Slough of Despond."

CHRISTIAN: I nearly sank.

HELP: If you'd looked, there are good and substantial steps through the midst of the slough.

CHRISTIAN: I saw them not.

HELP: Next time be better looking! Don't worry. Once through yond Little Gate the ground is good.

CHRISTIAN: Thanks for your help sir.

HELP: (*Shrugs.*) What choice have I? Help's me name.

(HELP *tips his hat and goes.* CHRISTIAN *watches him go. Meanwhile,* PLIABLE *arrives home, bumping into* OBSTINATE.)

OBSTINATE: Back so soon neighbour Pliable?

PLIABLE: Weren't for me.

OBSTINATE: Thou turncoat! Hang thee.

(OBSTINATE *slaps* PLIABLE.)

PLIABLE: Ow!

OBSTINATE: If thou thinkst to get further work from me – or any other neighbour – think better of it.

PLIABLE: This makes my condition seven times worse than if I'd continued my flight!

OBSTINATE: Dost not thou comprehend? I despise thee!

(OBSTINATE *turns his back on* PLIABLE *who runs dolefully away.* CHRISTIAN *walks on beneath the weight of his burden. Behind him,* CHRISTIANA *and the* CHILDREN *approach* OBSTINATE.)

CHRISTIANA: I heard a rumour neighbour Pliable's returned.

OBSTINATE: (*Nodding.*) Twice the fool that he departed.

CHRISTIANA: Any news of my husband?

OBSTINATE: Aye. Pliable left him floundering in a pile of stinking muck.

CHRISTIANA: Has he not also returned?

OBSTINATE: He's never likely to – as the biggest fool by a long chalk of the two.

(*Exit OBSTINATE. CHRISTIANA is devastated.*)

SON: Where is Father, Mother?

CHRISTIANA: Son, you have no father now.

DAUGHTER: Is Daddy never coming home?

CHRISTIANA: That is so.

(*The CHILDREN run off – the SON roaring angry and the DAUGHTER in tears, upset. CHRISTIANA sits down wearily and reflects, disappearing into the darkness.*)

*

3
MR WORLDLY WISEMAN

(MR WORLDLY WISEMAN *rushes towards* CHRISTIAN *bowed under the weight of his burden.*)

WISEMAN: How now good fellow? Whither away in a burdened manner?

CHRISTIAN: A burdened manner indeed! I tell you sir, I am going to yonder Little Gate. For there I shall be given a way to be rid of this heavy load.

WISEMAN: Hast thou no wife and children?

CHRISTIAN: I'm as if I had none.

WISEMAN: I'll give thee council. Wilt thou hearken?

CHRISTIAN: If it be good.

WISEMAN: With all speed rid thyself of thy burden!

CHRISTIAN: That's what I seek! But I can't get it off myself nor can any man take it off me. Therefore, go I this way to be rid of my burden.

WISEMAN: Who bade thee go this way?

CHRISTIAN: Evangelist.

WISEMAN: Beshrew him for his counsel! There is no more dangerous way in the world than that unto which he hath sent thee. I perceive thou hast already been mired in the Slough of Despond. That slough is but beginning of sorrows. Hear me – I am older than thee. In this way which thou goest thou art like to meet with: wearisomeness, painfulness, hunger perils nakedness, sword lions dragons darkness, and in a word death, and what not! Why should a man giving heed to a stranger so carelessly cast himself away?

CHRISTIAN: This burden upon my back's worse than all those things together sir.

WISEMAN: How camest thou by thy burden?

CHRISTIAN: By reading this book in my hand.

WISEMAN: I might have known! To thee it has happened as to other weak men who meddle in things too high. They run them upon desperate ventures, to get they know not what.

CHRISTIAN: I know what I would get: an ease from my burden!

WISEMAN: But why seek thou for thy ease in this way? Let me direct thee to thy desires minus these dangers, in a way wherein thou shalt meet with safety, friendship and content.

CHRISTIAN: Open this secret I pray you sir.

WISEMAN: Yonder is a village named Morality. In that village there dwells a gentleman: Mr Legality. His house is not a mile from here, and if he be not at home himself, he hath a pretty young son named Civility will do it as well as the old gent himself. There thou'll be eased of thy burden. A house thou might have at a reasonable rate. Provision there's good and cheap. Thou wilt be happy there – living by honest neighbours – in credit and good fashion.

CHRISTIAN: The way to this man's house?

WISEMAN: See yonder high hill?

CHRISTIAN: Too well.

WISEMAN: Go thou by that hill. First house thou'll come to is his.

CHRISTIAN: Thanks, many times sir for this.

WISEMAN: Assisting the lost is ever my chief bliss.

(MISTER WORLDLY WISEMAN *pats* CHRISTIAN *on the back, propelling him towards the hill. The sky darkens.* CHRISTIAN is *now alone, looking up at the high hill. Thunders begin to rumble. Flashes of fire come from the hill.* CHRISTIAN *shrinks as if the hill will fall on him.* MOSES *appears carrying two tablets of stone and he isn't happy.*)

MOSES: Thou shalt have no gods before me!

(CHRISTIAN *trembles. The hill appears to loom over him.*)

Thou shalt not make a likeness of anything.
Thou shalt not take the name of the Lord thy God in vain.
Remember the Sabbath, keeping it holy.
Honour thy father and mother.

(CHRISTIAN *nods in agreement to all this, all the time bowing as if under pressure.* MOSES *drops one of the tablets on* CHRISTIAN's *foot.*)

CHRISTIAN: Ow!

MOSES: Thou shalt not kill commit adultery or steal.
Thou shan't bear false witness.
Thou shalt not covet thy neighbour's ass.

CHRISTIAN: I wouldn't do that!

MOSES: Thou better had not.

(MOSES *drops the second tablet onto* CHRISTIAN's *other foot.*)

CHRISTIAN: Ow!

MOSES: Thou shalt not eat of them that chew the cud alone.

CHRISTIAN: I'll take care with my diet...

(MOSES *looms over* CHRISTIAN *who cowers on the ground.* EVANGELIST *appears.*)

EVANGELIST: Christian what dost thou here?

(At EVANGELIST's *appearance* MOSES *startles. The two stare each other out then* MOSES *leaves.* EVANGELIST *comes to* CHRISTIAN.)

Did not I direct thee to the Little Gate?

CHRISTIAN: Aye.

EVANGELIST: How is it that thou art so out of that way?

CHRISTIAN: A gentleman convinced me I might – in the village called Morality – be eased of my burden by Mr Legality.

EVANGELIST: Thou hast begun to reject the council of the Most High to the hazarding of thy perdition.

CHRISTIAN: O woe!

EVANGELIST: That Mister thou met is Worldly Wiseman, of the town of Carnal Policy. He savours the doctrine of this world. He seeketh to prevent my ways.

CHRISTIAN: For harkening to his council, I am a thousand fools!

EVANGELIST: Legality is a cheat! His son Civility's a hypocrite! Tricks to beguile thee of salvation.

CHRISTIAN: Sir is there hope left for me? May I still reach the Little Gate?

EVANGELIST: All manner of sin and blasphemy shall be forgiven. Be not faithless but believing.

(EVANGELIST *again points* CHRISTIAN *towards the Little Gate.* CHRISTIAN, *moved, walks forwards again.* EVANGELIST *recedes as the Little Gate appears. It is shaped as a heart. Over the gate is written:*

"Knock and it shall be opened to you."

CHRISTIAN *knocks several times.*)

CHRISTIAN: Will you open up to an undeserving rebel?

(*The door is opened by* GOOD WILL.)

GOOD WILL: I am willing to let thee in with all my heart.

(GOOD WILL *gives* CHRISTIAN *a sudden yank; the two then appear on the Little Gate's other side.* CHRISTIAN *breathy heavily in shock from the pull.*)

Good Will bids you right welcome.

(GOOD WILL *strokes* CHRISTIAN *lovingly, which calms him somewhat.*)

Look before thee: see this further road?

(CHRISTIAN *nods.*)

This is the route that thou must travel.

CHRISTIAN: May a stranger not lose his way?

GOOD WILL: Thou canst tell right from wrong can't thou?

CHRISTIAN: Yes... What please of my burden?

GOOD WILL: Bear it 'til it falls of itself from thy back. A little distance from here is the House of the Interpreter. Go hither. Excellent things he will show thee.

CHRISTIAN: O I thank thee.

GOOD WILL: I bid thee Godspeed Christian. Carry on down the road. The Interpreter's House awaits thee.

(GOOD WILL *sends* CHRISTIAN *along the road.*)

CHRISTIAN: For sure an Interpreter's the very thing I need! He might reveal some meaning to my dream...

*

4
THE HOUSE OF THE INTERPRETER

(CHRISTIAN *arrives at the* INTERPRETER's *house and knocks.*)

INTERPRETER: (*From within.*) Enter in!

(CHRISTIAN *enters and is greeted by the* INTERPRETER, *an imposing figure with a staff.*)

Welcome to my world.

CHRISTIAN: Good Will did tell me thou hadst things to show me.

INTERPRETER: Aye, profitable things. Look on this.

(The INTERPRETER *reveals an androgynous person, whose eyes are lifted to heaven, the best of books in his hand, the law of truth upon his lips and the world behind him. The person in the picture stands invitingly, a crown of gold upon his head.*)

CHRISTIAN: What means this?

INTERPRETER: The man in this picture is one of a thousand!
Children he begets and labours into life.
He unfolds many dark things to sinners.
He is our Lord's only authorized guide.

CHRISTIAN: A man who begets children?

INTERPRETER: A strange androgyny. Beyond dichotomy.

CHRISTIAN: Dichotomy?

INTERPRETER: Dichotomies such as these.

(*The* INTERPRETER *bangs his staff again. An* OLD MAN *enters sweeping. As he does so, dust flies into the air. He dusts* CHRISTIAN, *almost causing him to choke. The* INTERPRETER *bangs his staff. The* OLD MAN *sweeps the rest of the room as a* PIOUS MAID *emerges with a bucket and mop. She goes to* CHRISTIAN *and pours the bucket of water over his head. She moves on sprinkling in the* OLD MAN's *wake.*)

CHRISTIAN: (*Spluttering.*) What is the meaning of this?

INTERPRETER: The parlour they sweep is the heart of man.
The dust is his sins and inward corruptions.
He that began to sweep is the Law.
She that sprinkles is your Gospel teaching.
You swing as a pendulum 'twixt the two.
'Tween Passion and Patience. The old and the new.
The Devil strives to put out your fire.
Christ pours his oil on your pyre.

CHRISTIAN: Expound this matter more fully to me.

INTERPRETER: Watch this bravery.

(A STOUT MAN *approaches a Gate before which a* CLERK *is writing.*)

STOUT MAN: Set down my name sir.

CLERK: No.

(*The* STOUT MAN *is not having this, and so draws his sword. The* CLERK *notices and turns into a* SOLDIER *blocking the* STOUT MAN's *way with drawn sword. The* STOUT MAN *puts his helmet upon his head and rushes towards the* SOLDIER *who lays upon him with deadly force. The* STOUT MAN *is not at all discouraged and falls to cutting and hacking most fiercely. After he has received and given many wounds, he cuts his way through and presses forwards into the palace. The* STOUT MAN *stands before the Gate as a voice resounds from within.*)

VOICE: Come in! Come in!
Eternal glory thou shalt win.

(*The gate opens and the* STOUT MAN *enters, welcomed by androgynous* SHINING ONES. *As the*

Gate closes again CHRISTIAN *turns to face the* INTERPRETER.)

CHRISTIAN: Verily I know the meaning of this. Now I may go hence...

INTERPRETER: Stay 'til I have showed thee a little further.

(*The* INTERPRETER *bangs his staff and a* MAN IN AN IRON CAGE *is revealed.* CHRISTIAN *at the* INTERPRETER's *urging gingerly approaches the* MAN IN THE IRON CAGE.)

CHRISTIAN: What art thou?

IRON MAN: I am not what I was once.

CHRISTIAN: What was thou once?

IRON MAN: A flourishing professor of the Christian faith – both in my eyes and in the eyes of others.

CHRISTIAN: Well. But what now art thou?

IRON MAN: A man in despair, shut up in it.

CHRISTIAN: How camest this condition?

IRON MAN: I left off to watch and be sober. I laid the reins on the neck of my lusts. I sinned against the Light of the World. Grieved the Spirit. God has left me. I have so hardened my heart that I cannot repent.

(CHRISTIAN *turns to the* INTERPRETER.)

CHRISTIAN: Is there no hope for him?

INTERPRETER: Ask.

CHRISTIAN: (*To* IRON MAN.) Is there no hope but you must be kept in this iron cage?

IRON MAN: No hope.

CHRISTIAN: The Son of the Blessed is very pitiful.

IRON MAN: I have crucified Him in myself afresh.

(CHRISTIAN *backs away from the* MAN *in horror.*)

INTERPRETER: Be this man's misery an everlasting memory.

CHRISTIAN: Time to be on my way...

INTERPRETER: One further thing.

> (The INTERPRETER *bangs his staff heavily once. The* MAN IN THE IRON CAGE *disappears back behind the veil, to be replaced by a trembling* MAN ON A BED.)

CHRISTIAN: Why does this man tremble thus?

> (*The* MAN ON A BED *suddenly cries out.*)

BED MAN: This night as I was asleep, I dreamed: behold the heavens grew exceeding black, also thundered and lightened most fearful wise – put me in an agony! In my dream I looked up and saw the clouds rack at an unusual rate, upon which the great sound of a trumpet, and a Man sitting on a cloud with heaven's hoards. All were in flaming fire. Also, the heavens a burning flame! Then a voice:

"Arise ye dead and come to judgement."

Rocks rent. Graves opened. The dead came forth! Some were exceeding glad and looked upwards. Others sought to hide themselves under rocks. The Man on the cloud opened a great book and bid the whole world draw near. The fierce flame issued before him causing a distance as betwixt a judge and his prisoners. The Man on the cloud proclaimed to his crowd:

"Gather together the tares chaff and stubble and cast them into the lake which burns!" With that the bottomless pit opened whereabouts I stood. Out of its mouth came smoke and coals of fire a hideous din. Then said the Man:

"Gather my wheat in the garner."

Many were caught up and into the clouds. I was left to tarry. I sought to hide but no – the eye of the Man on the cloud was on me. My conscience accused me on every side. My sins were in my mind.

CHRISTIAN: What was it made you so afraid at this sight?

BED MAN: Isn't that obvious? I thought the day of judgement had arrived! That I would be into hell cast down.

(CHRISTIAN *turns to the* INTERPRETER.)

CHRISTIAN: That's enough of this.

(*The* INTERPRETER *bangs his staff. Two* SHINING ONES *emerge from the veil and gently pull the* MAN ON A BED *back behind.*)

INTERPRETER: Hast thou considered all these things?

CHRISTIAN: They put me in hope and fear.

INTERPRETER: Hope and fear are Vision!

(*The* INTERPRETER *produces a* DOVE.)

Good Christian
The Comforter always be with thee
To guide thee on the way to the City!

(*The* INTERPRETER *lets the* DOVE *fly as* CHRISTIAN *is seized by the spirit and sings.*)

CHRISTIAN: Here have I seen things rare and profitable:
Things pleasant, dreadful, things to make me stable
In what I have begun to take in hand:
Then let me dwell on them and understand
Just what I have seen and let me be
Grateful good Interpreter to thee.

INTERPRETER: Now hast one reached where two are true:

Humanity and Divinity in you!

(The INTERPRETER *reveals the Cross.* CHRISTIAN *drops to his knees in awe. His burden is loosed from his shoulders and falls from his back. The* INTERPRETER *takes it away.* CHRISTIAN *weeps for joy.* THREE SHINING ONES *appear to* CHRISTIAN.)

1ST SHINING: Peace be to thee! Thy sins are forgiven thee.

SHINING ONES: Gloria Hallelujah.

(The THREE SHINING ONES *strip* CHRISTIAN *of his rags.)*

2ND SHINING: Away with these rags! New raiment thou shalt wear.

SHINING ONES: Gloria Hallelujah.

(The THREE SHINING ONES *dress* CHRISTIAN *in new raiment.)*

3RD SHINING: I give you this roll! Your Eternal identity.

SHINING ONES: Hallelujah! Gloria!

(The 3RD SHINING ONE *has given* CHRISTIAN *a roll.* CHRISTIAN *writhes in ecstasy again singing.)*

CHRISTIAN: Thus far did I come laden with my sin
Nor could aught ease the grief that I was in.
Till I came here. What a place is this!
It must be the beginning of my bliss.

(CHRISTIAN *stands transfigured.* CHRISTIANA *enters.)*

CHRISTIANA: My husband I have heard is much transformed. His wishes begin to be fulfilled. His burden is took. He struts around town. Giving out pieces of his mind. Dreams he is perfect. Can it be true?

(CHRISTIANA *leaves and* CHRISTIAN *comes down from his ecstasy.)*

*

5
THE LESSON AT THE ARBOUR

(*The cross disappears and* CHRISTIAN *turns once more to the road. The* SHINING ONES *shed their garments of light and are transformed into three men asleep on the ground. These are* SIMPLE, SLOTH *and* PRESUMPTION. CHRISTIAN *looks upon them lying at his feet.*)

CHRISTIAN: Why here are three that sleep on the top of a mast. Awake! The dead sea is under you! If he that goes like a roaring lion comes by, you'll become prey to his teeth. Awake. Awake! Awake!!!

SIMPLE: I see no danger.

SLOTH: Yet a little more sleep.

PRESUMPTION: Every tub must stand on its own bottom.

CHRISTIAN: In this wise thou'll not prove true by the end of the way.

SIMPLE: Which way?

SLOTH: Leave me sleep.

PRESUMPTION: Look to thyself!

CHRISTIAN: Swine love their sty.

(CHRISTIAN *walks on past* SIMPLE, SLOTH *and* PRESUMPTION.)

I see that I have only me to talk with.
I have my roll on which is my Eternal Identity.
I feel refreshed each time it I read.

(*A stream runs before* CHRISTIAN's *feet. He smiles and stoops to drink. As he looks up he sees a great hill looming. He baulks at the sight of it then steels himself.* CHRISTIAN *begins to climb the Hill Difficulty.*)

Better though difficult the right way to go,

Than wrong way but easy and end in woe.

(*The going is arduous and soon* CHRISTIAN *is clambering on his hands and knees due to the steepness.*)

Though my spirit covets to ascend
My flesh is weak and craves to rest.

(CHRISTIAN *comes to an Arbour. His face lights up in delight. Ethereal voices sound around* CHRISTIAN.)

VOICES: Rest your bones. Take the weight off your feet. Read relax and sleep.

(CHRISTIAN *enters the Arbour as lulling music sounds. He reads from his roll until his eyes begin to droop. He falls into a slumber and his roll drops from his hand. He is fast asleep. Another* PILGRIM *struggles up Hill Difficulty and passes the Arbour. The* PILGRIM *sees* CHRISTIAN *sleeping. He tuts, very disapprovingly. He approaches* CHRISTIAN *in the Arbour.*)

PILGRIM: Go to the ant thou sluggard. Consider her ways!

(CHRISTIAN *starts up. The other* PILGRIM *gives him a disapproving look then leaves.*)

CHRISTIAN: Mind your own nose!

(CHRISTIAN *glares after the* PILGRIM *then realises it is getting late.*)

Better go.

(CHRISTIAN *sets off again up the Hill Difficulty. The Arbour recedes as* CHRISTIAN *climbs. Two men,* TIMOROUS *and* MISTRUST, *suddenly come running against him furiously.*)

TIMOROUS: Help!

MISTRUST: Flee for your lives!

CHRISTIAN: Sirs, you run the wrong way!

TIMOROUS: Be afraid.

MISTRUST: Be very afraid!

TIMOROUS: O we were off to Zion's city. The farther we go the more danger we meet.

MISTRUST: Lions! They'd pull us to bits!!!

CHRISTIAN: Towards what security should I fly? Backwards is brimstone and fire!
The Celestial City equals safety.

(TIMOROUS *and* MISTRUST *run down the Hill.* CHRISTIAN *looks ahead in fear. He feels in his bosom for his roll.*)

A look at my roll shall comfort me.

(*It is not there.*)

O wretched silly! I've lost me Eternal identity!

(So CHRISTIAN *wearily retraces his steps, sighing and weeping.*)

That I should indulge the flesh in the midst of trouble! O that I had not kipped!

(*The Arbour comes back into view.* CHRISTIAN *rushes into it and finds his roll.*)

O the Lord is abundantly merciful!

(CHRISTIAN *weeps then pulls himself together, leaves the Arbour for a second time and climbs on.* CHRISTIANA *appears.*)

CHRISTIANA: Off learning truths about yourself. I learn how to mope home alone.

(*She disappears again.*)

*

6
PALACE BEAUTIFUL

(CHRISTIAN *climbs on. Night is falling. Noises sound from doleful creatures. Two* LIONS *appear before* CHRISTIAN. *He shrieks. The* LIONS *growl but do not approach him.* CHRISTIAN *stops moving forwards. The voice of The* PORTER *calls to him.*)

PORTER: Is thy strength so small? Fear not the lions for they are chained and placed there for a trial of faith and the discovery of those that have none. Keep in the midst of the path and no hurt shall come to thee.

(CHRISTIAN *braces himself and – in fear and trembling – passes the* LIONS. *They roar but do him no harm. As he passes them, a stately palace comes into view. The* PORTER *meets* CHRISTIAN.)

CHRISTIAN: What house is this sir?

PORTER: Why, 'tis Palace Beautiful.

CHRISTIAN: May I lodge here tonight?

PORTER: What's thy name?

CHRISTIAN: At first it was Graceless but now Christian is my name. I'm of the race of Japheth whom God shall persuade to dwell in the tents of Shem.

(PORTER *is delighted.*)

PORTER: A Godly conceit! For thou knowest that Japheth is an emblem of the mind of Man which God shall expand into the tents of Shem: the Life Spiritual. Thou hast spent thy time in wise study. Ye are bid welcome and come in.

(CHRISTIAN *enters into Palace Beautiful. Three damsels – PRUDENCE, PIETY and CHARITY – sit in the parlour and turn to greet the newly arrived.*)

These damsels will take excellent care of thee. They be Piety, Prudence and Charity. All three here abide beloved of the Lord but the greatest of these is Charity.

(PORTER *exits chuckling.* CHRISTIAN *turns to the damsels.*)

CHARITY: Come in and sit with us.

(CHRISTIAN *sits with them.*)

PRUDENCE: A thimble of wine?

CHRISTIAN: That is most kind.

CHARITY: Supper will be done in a short time.

(CHRISTIAN *smiles.*)

PIETY: Come good Christian. Since we have been so loving to you I hope that you will discourse with us.

CHRISTIAN: I'd be most glad to.

PIETY: Art thou a married man?

CHRISTIAN: A wife, a boy, and a girl child.

PRUDENCE: Why are they not with you?

CHRISTIAN: Would they were! They were utterly averse to my going on pilgrimage.

CHARITY: If you had tried to show them the danger of staying...

CHRISTIAN: So I did but they would in no wise believe.

PIETY: Did you pray God He would bless your counsel to them?

CHRISTIAN: Yes with much affection, for you must know my wife and brood are dear to me.

CHARITY: What could they say for themselves, why they came not?

CHRISTIAN: My wife's afraid of losing this world. My children are given to youth's dumb enjoyments. What with one thing and what with another, they left me alone and wandering.

(CHARITY *places a hand on* CHRISTIAN's *shoulder. This cheers him.*)

PRUDENCE: Do you not think sometimes of the country from which you hail?

CHRISTIAN: With shame and detestation. I now desire a better country: that is a heavenly.

PRUDENCE: Do you bear with you some bad things still?

CHRISTIAN: Greatly against my will. Especially my inward and carnal thinking. Those things are my grief and might I but choose I would never more think of them. For when I would be doing of that which is best, that which is the worst is within me.

CHARITY: Do you not find sometimes as if those things were overcome which at other times are such a perplexity?

CHRISTIAN: Yes, but seldom. The hours in which I have a Godly mind are golden.

PRUDENCE: What is it that makes Mount Zion your desire?

CHRISTIAN: There I hope to see my Lord alive! There I hope to be rid of annoyances. There they say there is no death. There I shall dwell with wonderful company. For to tell you truth I love Him because I was eased of my burden by Him, and I am weary of sickness within. I would fain be where I'll die no more, with the company that cries continually "holy, holy, holy!"

(*Bells sound.* CHRISTIAN *is startled at this.*)

PRUDENCE: Which merely means that supper is prepared.

(PRUDENCE *and* PIETY *exit.* CHRISTIAN *rises as* CHARITY *lays the table.* CHRISTIAN *helps her.* PRUDENCE *and* PIETY *re-enter with a fat meal. They all gather round the table and as* PIETY *say grace.*)

PIETY:　　　Our thanks be to Him that built this house
　　　　　　Who hath fought and slain the power of death
　　　　　　That hath made many pilgrims princes
　　　　　　Who were from the dunghill bred.

　　　　　　(*They settle down to feast as night draws in. Far away from the Palace Beautiful*, CHRISTIANA *has supper ready for her* CHILDREN.)

CHRISTIANA:　(*Calling.*) Dinner children!

　　　　　　(SON *and* DAUGHTER *enter.*)

SON:　　　　What we got tonight?

CHRISTIANA:　Stew.

SON:　　　　Had stew the last three nights.

DAUGHTER:　Not feeling hungry.

CHRISTIANA:　You'll eat what's put in front of you.

SON:　　　　Why in hell should I?

DAUGHTER:　I'm not eating none of this muck!

　　　　　　(*The* CHILDREN *storm out.* CHRISTIANA *collapses in tears.*)

CHRISTIANA:　Bread of sorrows is my repast.

　　　　　　(*At the Palace Beautiful, the meal is eaten.*)

PRUDENCE:　Sufficient?

CHRISTIAN:　That was wonderful, thank you.

　　　　　　(PRUDENCE *and* PIETY *clear the table and its contents away.*)

CHARITY:　　It is time we took ourselves to rest. We have the upper chamber named Peace prepared for you. Wherein thou shalt sleep 'til break of day.

　　　　　　(CHARITY *takes* CHRISTIAN *into the chamber called Peace. She leaves, and* CHRISTIAN *settles himself in the bed and drifts to a gentle sleep.*)

CHRISTIAN: And so I dream that I'm utterly forgiven
And dwell already next door to heaven.
My dream is that this is my Lord's doing.

(CHRISTIAN *sleeps a good night's sleep. The sun comes up.* CHRISTIAN *rises with the sun.* PIETY, PRUDENCE *and* CHARITY *enter.*)

CHARITY: Before you go we wish to show you the house's rarities.

CHRISTIAN: I'd dearly love to see them.

PIETY: To the study!

(PIETY *shows* CHRISTIAN *into the study.*)

Here keep we records of oldest antiquity.

(PIETY *produces various scrolls.*)

This be the pedigree of the Lord of the Hill. See He is Son of the Ancient of Days and comes by Eternal generation. Here be fully recorded His acts and the names of his army of hundreds. This tells of the worthy deeds some of his servants have performed. How they subdued kingdoms, wrought righteousness, obtained promises, stopped the mouths of lions, quenched the violence of fire, escaped the sword, waxed valiant in fight and turned to fight the throngs of the alien.

(*Now* PRUDENCE *comes to* CHRISTIAN.)

PRUDENCE: Now to our armoury!

(PRUDENCE *takes* CHRISTIAN *into the armoury.*)

Behold the instruments by which His servants have done things wonderful.

(PRUDENCE *handles various weapons.*)

Moses' rod. The hammer and nail with which Jeal slew Sisera. The jawbone with which Samson did feats a-mighty. This the sling and stone with which

David Goliath slew. And here the sword with which our Lord will kill the man of sin in that day He shall rise up to the prey.

(CHRISTIAN *gazes upon all these with awe.* CHARITY *now appears with armour.*)

CHARITY: We wrestle not against flesh and blood but against spiritual wickedness.

(*The three* MAIDENS *dress* CHRISTIAN *in armour.*)

Therefore take unto you the armour of God. Have your loins girt about with Truth. Have on you the breastplate of Righteousness. Let your feet be shod with the gospel of Peace. Above all take the shield of Faith, Salvation's helmet and the sword of the Spirit which is the Word of the Lord.

(CHRISTIAN *being now armoured, the damsels stand back from him. All three speak in unison.*)

DAMSELS: You see in the distance a pleasant country, beauteous with vineyard and woods, fruits and flowers, springs and fountains scrumptious to behold.

CHRISTIAN: What name is that country's?

DAMSELS: Immanuel's Land. When there thou comest thou mayest see the gate of the Celestial City, as the shepherds that live thereby shall reveal.

CHRISTIAN: Onwards to the Land of Immanuel!

DAMSELS: As difficult as it was coming up, it is dangerous coming down. It is a hard descent to the Valley of Humiliation...

(CHARITY, PIETY, PRUDENCE *recede.*)

*

7
TWO VALLEYS

(*The sky is grey and* CHRISTIAN *shivers in the Valley of Humiliation. He is but a little way in when he spies a foul fiend coming across the field to meet him. This is* APOLLYON – *a monster hideous to behold. He is clothed with scales like a fish, he has wings like a dragon, feet like a bear, out of his belly comes fire and smoke and his mouth is as the mouth of a lion.* CHRISTIAN *shakes as he stands his ground.*)

APOLLYON: Whence came ye and whither are ye bound?

CHRISTIAN: I am from the City of Destruction and am going to Zion's Town.

APOLLYON: I perceive thou art one of my subjects – the City of Destruction is mine. I am prince and god of it. How is't thou runs away from thy king? Were it not that I hope thou mayest do me more service, I should with one blow strike thee to the ground.

CHRISTIAN: I was born in your dominions. Your service was hard and your wages death.

APOLLYON: No prince will lightly lose subjects. Be content to go back.

CHRISTIAN: I have let myself to another. How can I go back with thee and not be for treason hanged?

APOLLYON: Thou didst the same to me and yet I'll willingly pass by it.

CHRISTIAN: I promised thee before I came of age. The Prince under whose banner I now stand is able to absolve me, yea and to pardon also what I did in compliance to thee. Besides O thou destroying Apollyon to speak the truth I like his service, his wages, his servants, his government, his company, and his country all better than thine. Therefore leave off persuasion. I follow Him.

APOLLYON: Thou already hast been unfaithful in thy service to him.

CHRISTIAN: O Apollyon wherein have I been unfaithful?

APOLLYON: Thou didst faint at thy first setting out. Thou almost choked in the Gulf of Despond. Didst try erroneous ways to be rid of thy burden. Thou wrongfully slept and lost thy choice thing. Almost went back at the sight of the lions. Thou art desirous within of vain-glory in all that thou doest or sayest.

CHRISTIAN: And much more thou hast left out! The Prince whom I serve and honour is forgiving.

APOLLYON: This Prince is my enemy! I am come out on purpose to withstand thee.

CHRISTIAN: Apollyon take heed of thyself for this is the King's highway.

APOLLYON: I swear by my infernal den that thou shalt go no further. I am void of fear in this matter. Here will I spill thy soul.

(*They fight.* APOLLYON *wounds* CHRISTIAN *on his head.* CHRISTIAN *gives some back.* APOLLYON *follows his work furiously.* CHRISTIAN *resists as manfully as he can. This sore combat almost spends* CHRISTIAN *until by reason of his wounds he grows very weak.* APOLLYON *gives* CHRISTIAN *a dreadful fall and wrestles him to the ground.* APOLLYON *almost presses* CHRISTIAN *to death.*)

APOLLYON: I am sure of thee now!

(*As* APOLLYON *prepares to make an end of* CHRISTIAN *the latter nimbly reaches for his sword and cries out.*)

CHRISTIAN: Rejoice not against me mine enemy. When I fall I rise again!

(CHRISTIAN *gives a deadly thrust. APOLLYON staggers back.*)

Through Him that loves us in all things we're more than conquerors.

(APOLLYON *spreads forth his dragon's wings, and speeds away.* CHRISTIAN *kneels to pray.*)

I here give thanks to him that hath delivered me out of the mouth of the lion. Thanks and blessed always be His holiest name.

(CHRISTIAN *wearily gets up. It is dark.* CHRISTIAN, *tired and wounded, divests himself of his armour then limps on, into the Valley of the Shadow of Death. The* DREAMER *describes the scene.*)

Now enter I a wilderness
A land of deserts and pits
A land of drought
A Valley of the shadow of death.

(CHRISTIAN *presses on into the desert which lies before him. It has grown very dark.*)

Deliver me out of the mire and let me sink not.

(*A sudden sound of awful moaning. Before* CHRISTIAN *appears the Mouth of Hell. Flame and smoke come out in abundance, with sparks and hideous noises.*)

O Lord I beseech Thee deliver my soul!

(*Doleful voices lament.* CHRISTIAN *is nothing but a shadow as he attempts to make his way past the terrible maw. Ghostly figures of* DEMONS *run out of the mouth and rush around* CHRISTIAN, *almost tearing him to pieces or trampling him down.* CHRISTIAN *continues to mumble prayers.*)

Deliver me O Lord please deliver me.

(*The* DEMONS *give back and retreat into the mouth of Hell.* CHRISTIAN *presses on. A sly* HOBGOBLIN *emerges from the mouth, in appearance just like* CHRISTIAN. *He walks beside the pilgrim and speaks in* CHRISTIAN's *voice.*)

HOBGOBLIN: Cursed be that god who brought me here.

CHRISTIAN: Who sayeth that?

HOBGOBLIN: Know not you your own voice?

CHRISTIAN: Merciful God!

HOBGOBLIN: Such are his rewards. This God of thine is the Devil.

CHRISTIAN: That I should so disrespect my Lord!

HOBGOBLIN: Let Christ go. Let him go. Let him go.

CHRISTIAN: No never no!

HOBGOBLIN: He's gone. The Lord has abandoned thee.

CHRISTIAN: This is not I. I would never think such things. A demon sent to tempt me...

HOBGOBLIN: I will cool thee insensibly, by degree, a little by little. What care though I be seven years your heart a-chilling. Continual rocking lulls a crying child.

CHRISTIAN: Satan get thee behind me!

(*The voice of another pilgrim sounds from far off.*)

FAITHFUL: Yea though I walk through the valley of the shadow of death I fear no Evil. Thou art with me. Thy rod and thy staff comfort me.

CHRISTIAN: The Lord is my Shepherd. Thou art not!

(*The* HOBGOBLIN *disappears.* CHRISTIAN *prays intensely.*)

Show me thy ways Lord. Show me The Way!

(CHRISTIAN *is seized by an Inspiration.*)

I seek for Him that maketh the seven stars and Orion.
Who turneth the shadow of death into morning.

(*A* SHINING ONE *enters and gives* CHRISTIAN *a laying-on- of-hands healing.*)

SHINING ONE: By His light through darkness you may go.

(CHRISTIAN *sings.*)

CHRISTIAN: O world of wonders! – I can say no less -
That I should be preserved in that distress
That I have met with here! O blessed be
The hand that from it hath delivered me.
Dangers in darkness devils hell and sin
Did compass me while I this vale was in:
Yea snares and pits and traps and nets did lie
My path about that worthless silly I
Might have been caught entangled and cast down
But since I live let Jesu wear the crown!

(*The* SHINING ONE *helps* CHRISTIAN *to his feet.* CHRISTIAN *laughs for joy as he watches The* SHINING ONE *go.*)

*

8
CHRISTIAN, FAITHFUL AND TALKATIVE

(*Another pilgrim,* FAITHFUL, *appears making his way along the road ahead of* CHRISTIAN. CHRISTIAN *calls to him.*)

CHRISTIAN: Ho ho! So-ho! I will be your companion.

(FAITHFUL *looks behind him.*)

Stay, stay 'til I come up to you!

FAITHFUL: No, the Avenger of Blood is behind me!

(FAITHFUL *hurries on.* CHRISTIAN *begins to run and soon catches up with* FAITHFUL, *passing him.*)

CHRISTIAN: See the book is true: the first shall be last.

(CHRISTIAN *laughs vain-gloriously.* FAITHFUL *smiles indulgently.* CHRISTIAN *stumbles and falls.* FAITHFUL *rushes to help him. They have a good laugh together.*)

CHRISTIAN: I am glad that I have caught up with you. I heard your voice in the valley. I am Christian.

FAITHFUL: Glad to hear it. Faithful I am.

(*They vigorously shake hands.*)

CHRISTIAN: From whence dost thou hail?

FAITHFUL: Destruction City.

CHRISTIAN: Same as I! I should be very glad to travel with you.

FAITHFUL: Nothing would please me more.

(*They hug.*)

CHRISTIAN: Let us swap edifying stories of ourselves what we've met upon the way as we travel onwards.

FAITHFUL: An excellent proposal.

CHRISTIAN: I'll wager it happened with you as with me on your leaving the Destruction City: you fell into the Slough of Despond.

FAITHFUL: I got to the Little Gate without dipping into that mire, only I met with one named Wanton.

CHRISTIAN: Not her!

FAITHFUL: You cannot think what a flattering tongue she hath unless you've met her. She promised me all manner of content.

CHRISTIAN: Except the content of a good conscience.

FAITHFUL: All carnal and fleshy content.

CHRISTIAN: The abhorred of the Lord fall in her ditch. Thank God you escaped.

FAITHFUL: I know not whether I did wholly escape her or no.

CHRISTIAN: You never consented to her desires?!

FAITHFUL: No! No. Not so much as to defile myself. I remembered an old writing I'd seen: "Her steps take hold to hell." So I shut mine eyes against her looks bewitching me. Then she railed at me and I went on my way.

CHRISTIAN: You met with no other assault as you came?

FAITHFUL: When I came to the foot of Hill Difficulty, I met a very agéd man. He questioned me. I told him I was bound for the Celestial City. So said he "Thou lookst an honest fellow. Wilt thou be content to dwell for my wages with me?" I asked him his name and where dwelt he. He said his name was Adam the first and that he dwelt in the town of Deceit. I asked him then what was his work? What the wages he gave? "My work has many delights and my wages are that ye should be my heir at the last." I further asked what house kept he, and what other servants had he? "My house is maintained with all the dainties in the world, and my servants are those of my own begetting." I asked, what children had he? "I have three lovely daughters:

the lust of the flesh, the lust of the eyes, and the pride of life. You can marry all of them if you like!" I asked him how long time he would have me live with him? And he told me "as long as I'm alive."

CHRISTIAN: To what conclusion came you and the old man at last?

FAITHFUL: Why at first I found myself inclined to go with him for I thought he spoke very fair. But glancing at his forehead as we talked, I saw written there: "Put off the old man with his deeds."

CHRISTIAN: What happened then?

FAITHFUL: It came burning hot in my mind: whatever he said, however he flattered, when he got me home to his house he would enslave me. I bid him forbear to talk with me, nor would I come near the door of his house. So he reviled me and told me he'd make my way bitter to my soul. After that I turned to depart from him but just as I turned I felt him take hold of my flesh and give me a deadly twitch back. I thought he had pulled part of me after him! "O wretched man!" I cried as I went on my way up the hill. When I got halfway up I looked behind me and saw one following swift as the wind. So he overtook me just about the place where the bench stands.

CHRISTIAN: There did I sit down to rest and – being overcome with sleep – I lost this roll from my bosom...

FAITHFUL: Good brother, hear me: when the man overtook me, he knocked me and laid me out for dead. When I came to myself, I asked him wherefore thus he served me? He said because of my secret inclining towards that first Adam. With that he beat me down backward so I lay at his foot again dead. When I came to myself again, I cried him mercy but he said "I know not how to show mercy!" Then down he knocked me a third time! Doubtless he'd have made an end of me but one came by and bade him forbear.

CHRISTIAN: Who was it that made him forbear?

FAITHFUL: He was our Lord.

(*They smile at each other, touched.*)

CHRISTIAN: That man who beat you was Moses. He shows no mercy to lawbreakers. How went the rest of your journey?

FAITHFUL: I had sunshine the rest of the way. Even through the Valley of the Shadow of Death.

CHRISTIAN: Wish I could say the same.

FAITHFUL: Tell me about it.

(CHRISTIAN *is about to oblige when* FAITHFUL *spots where a man whose name is* TALKATIVE *is walking at a distance beside them.*)

Look: another pilgrim.

CHRISTIAN: It may be.

(FAITHFUL *calls to* TALKATIVE.)

FAITHFUL: Friend, whither away? Are you going to the heavenly country?

TALKATIVE: I am going to that same place.

FAITHFUL: I hope we may have your good company.

TALKATIVE: With my very good will.

FAITHFUL: Come on, let us together.

(TALKATIVE *comes to* FAITHFUL *and* CHRISTIAN.)

Let us spend our time in discoursing of things that have profit.

TALKATIVE: To talk of good things is very acceptable to me.

(The three begin to journey together. The SHINING ONES *watch.)*

To speak the truth, there are but few that care to spend their time in so good a work but choose rather to be speaking of things to no profit. This hath troubled me.

FAITHFUL: What things are so worthy of the use of the tongue than the things of the God of heaven?

TALKATIVE: I like you wonderful well, for your mouth's full of conviction. What thing is so pleasant and profitable as to talk of the things of God? For instance, if a man doth delight to talk of the history-mystery, or if a man doth love to talk of signs and miracles and wonders – where shall he find things so sweetly penned as in the Scripture Holy?

FAITHFUL: To be profited by such things in our talk must be our design.

TALKATIVE: That's what I said! For by so doing a man may get knowledge of many things. The vanity of the earthly. The benefit of things above. More particularly a man may learn of the necessity of the new birth, the insufficiency of works, the need of Christ's righteousness and so on. A man may learn to refute false opinions. To vindicate truth! Also instruct poor ignorance.

FAITHFUL: Glad to hear these things from you.

TALKATIVE: All's not of works but of grace!!!

FAITHFUL: What shall we now talk of?

TALKATIVE: I will talk of things heavenly or things earthly. Things moral or things evangelical. Things sacred or things profane. Things past. Things to come. Things foreign. Things at home. Things more essential. Things circumstantial. Provided all be profitable!

(*Whilst* TALKATIVE *is saying the above* CHRISTIAN *has motioned to* FAITHFUL *to stay behind a bit.* FAITHFUL *and* CHRISTIAN *talk aside about* TALKATIVE.)

FAITHFUL: Why what a brave companion we've got! This man makes an excellent pilgrim.

CHRISTIAN: He will beguile twenty that know him not.

FAITHFUL: Do you know him?

CHRISTIAN: Better than he knows himself.

FAITHFUL: Pray what is he?

CHRISTIAN: He is the son of one Say-well who dwelt in Prating-row and he is known to all as Talkative of Prating-row. Notwithstanding his fancy tongue, he is a sorry fellow.

FAITHFUL: He seems a very pretty man.

CHRISTIAN: Near home he is ugly enough.

FAITHFUL: I am ready to think you jest.

CHRISTIAN: God forbid I'd jest or accuse one falsely! This man is for any company and for any talk. As he talks now with you, so he will in the alehouse. The more drink is in his belly, the more are these things in his mouth. Religion hath no place in his heart or house. All he hath lieth on his tongue. His religion is to make a racket.

FAITHFUL: In this man greatly deceived have I been.

CHRISTIAN: Bear in mind the proverb: "They say and do not." He is the very reproach, stain, and shame of religion. The people say of him: "A saint abroad and a devil at home." His poor family finds it so. He is such a churl, such a railer, so unreasonable with his servants that they know not how to take him. 'Tis better to deal with the Turk than he!

FAITHFUL: I am bound to believe thee.

CHRISTIAN: He thinks that hearing and saying will make a good Christian. He deceives his own soul. Hearing is but as the sowing of seed. Talking is not sufficient to prove that fruit's in the life in the heart. At the day of doom men shall be judged on their fruits.

FAITHFUL: This brings to my mind that of Moses! He describes the beast that is clean. Such a one parts the hoof and chews cud. Not one or only the other. The hare chews the cud but yet is unclean: he parts not the hoof! This truly resembles your Talkative: he chews the cud, he seeks knowledge, he chews upon the word but he divides not the hoof. He parts not the way of sinners. As the hare, he retains the foot of a doe, and is therefore unclean.

CHRISTIAN: Sounding brass and tinkling symbols!

(*The two of them laugh about* TALKATIVE.)

FAITHFUL: I was not so fond of his company from the first. Now I am heartily sick of it. What shall we do to get rid?

CHRISTIAN: Do as I bid.

FAITHFUL: What'll that be?

CHRISTIAN: Go to him and ask him plain: whether true religion be set up in his conversation, his heart or his home.

(*They agree.* FAITHFUL *steps forward to* TALKATIVE.)

FAITHFUL: Come, what cheer? How is it with thee?

TALKATIVE: Well, thankee. I thought we should have had a great deal of talk by now.

FAITHFUL: If you will, we will fall to it pronto. The question is this: How does God's saving grace show itself in the heart of man?

TALKATIVE: A very good question. I shall willingly answer you thus: First, Where the grace of God is in the heart it causes great outcry against sin. Secondly…

FAITHFUL: Nay hold. Let us consider one at once. I think you should rather say: grace shows itself by making the soul abhor its sin.

TALKATIVE: What difference is there between crying out against sin and abhorring it?

FAITHFUL: O a very great deal! I've heard many cry against sin in the pulpit, who yet can abide it well enough in their conversation and heart and abode. Some cry out against sin even as Mummy cries against her child calling it "slut" and "naughty girl" then falling to hugging and kissing it.

TALKATIVE: You're trying to catch me out.

FAITHFUL: I am for setting things right. What is the second thing whereby you see work of grace in the heart?

TALKATIVE: Great knowledge of Gospel mysteries.

FAITHFUL: This should've been first! But first or last 'tis false. You may know like an angel and yet be no Christian.

TALKATIVE: This isn't for edification. You're trying to catch me out again.

FAITHFUL: If you please, propound another sign by which grace shows itself.

TALKATIVE: Not I. I see that we'll not agree.

CHRISTIAN: May I answer?

TALKATIVE: Use your liberty.

CHRISTIAN: A work of grace in the soul discovers itself to him that hath it thus: it gives him conviction of sin, chiefly in his nature's defilement – for the sake of which he is sure to be damned – if he finds not mercy by faith in Jesus. According to the strength and weakness of his faith, so is his joy and peace.

(TALKATIVE *squirms.*)

The grace of God within one is also shown to others thus: One by a confession of his faith in Christ. Two by a life fitting that confession. It is not seen by talk only – as a hypocrite or talkative person may show – but by a practical subjection in faith and love to the power of the Word. Now sir, if you object to this go ahead and object. If not then give me leave to propound a second question.

TALKATIVE: My part I see is to hear and not to object.

CHRISTIAN: My question is this: Do you experience the first part of this description? Doth your life and talk confirm the same? Or standeth your religion only in word or tongue but not in truth and deed?

(TALKATIVE *blushes.*)

TALKATIVE: You come now to experience, to conscience, and to God. This kind of discourse I did not count upon. Nor am I disposed to answer. I refuse to make you my judge. Pray, why do you ask me such questions?

FAITHFUL: (*To* CHRISTIAN.) Shall I?

CHRISTIAN: Go on.

FAITHFUL: Because we saw you so forward to talk and because we observed you had nought else but notion. Because we have heard that you are a man whose religion lies only in chat. They say you're a spot among Christians. Religion fares the worse for you. Your religion and an ale-house and covetousness and uncleanness and swearing and lying and vain company keeping are one. The proverb which is said of a whore is true of you:

to wit that "she is a shame to all women." You are a shame to us.

TALKATIVE: Since you are ready to take up reports and to judge thus rashly, I cannot but conclude that you are melancholy peevish men, not fit to talk with. I take my adieu.

(TALKATIVE *hurries away in tears.* CHRISTIAN *and* FAITHFUL *collapse into cackling.*)

CHRISTIAN: I told you that would happen! Our words and his lusts could not agree. He'd rather leave our company than reform he. Let him go. The loss is no man's but his own. He has saved us the trouble of slinging him from us.

FAITHFUL: I am grateful we had this talk with him. It may happen that he will think of it again. We have plainly dealt with him. If he perish our hands are clean of his blood.

*

9
EVANGELIST'S PROPHECY AND MERCY

(CHRISTIANA *is alone at home.*)

CHRISTIANA: I'd never have dreamed you could become this harsh judger of others. All this from one who abandons and discards his own family. I'd never have dreamed your dreams could be thus far from mine.

(CHRISTIANA *weeps at her sad plight. A knock on the door.*)

Who be?

MERCY: Your neighbour Mercy.

CHRISTIANA: Do come in.

(*Enter* MERCY.)

You are most welcome good neighbour Mercy.

MERCY: How do you?

CHRISTIANA: How should I do? I have a husband God knows where! Two children I can scarcely feed. Beneath my breasts is a broken heart filled to the brim with resentment.

MERCY: Being cracked, your heart will soon spill that. Be glad: at least your husband left you not for another.

CHRISTIANA: That's one thing, I suppose.

MERCY: By all accounts he is now more content.

CHRISTIANA: He certainly is now a man content to condemn others.

MERCY: His God has means to teach your husband the right road.

(MERCY *smiles reassuringly at a doubtful* CHRISTIANA.

On the road, EVANGELIST *appears before the Pilgrims.*)

EVANGELIST: Peace be with you, dearly beloved, and peace to your helpers!

CHRISTIAN: Good Evangelist!

FAITHFUL: Welcome a thousand times!

EVANGELIST: I am glad to see thee both.

(EVANGELIST *hugs them.*)

I hear you have been through many trials and have been the victors, and that you have – despite weaknesses – stayed in The Way to this day. The incorruptible crown is before you. That you might obtain it: run!

CHRISTIAN: That we will.

FAITHFUL: That we do.

EVANGELIST: You are not yet out of the devil's gunshot. You yet do more talk than fight. You've not resisted unto death. Let the Kingdom be always before you. Set your faces like flints. All power in heaven and earth's on your side!

CHRISTIAN: We know you are a prophet. Can you tell us of what might happen?

EVANGELIST: By and by you will come to a town. Therein many enemies will beset you. They will kill you. Be sure that one of you or both be faithful unto the end.

(CHRISTIAN *and* FAITHFUL *look forwards with trepidation. Back at home,* CHRISTIANA *is still talking with* MERCY.)

CHRISTIANA: My husband sees this world as somewhere to be abandoned. It's certainly a place I feel abandoned in.

MERCY: You've never thought to follow him?

CHRISTIANA: I cannot entertain such frivolous thinking. I have a family. If you'll excuse me, I must get ready. I promised to take the children to the fair.

(SON *and* DAUGHTER *rush in, excited.*)

CHILDREN: The fair! Fun fair!

(CHRISTIANA *takes their hands and moves away from* MERCY. MERCY *kneels to pray.*

On the Way CHRISTIAN *and* FAITHFUL *stand terrified before* EVANGELIST, *quavering at the road ahead of them.*)

EVANGELIST: Remember your friend. Believe steadfastly. Quit yourselves like men. Commit the keeping of your souls unto God your belovéd, whose name is Faithful and True.

(FAITHFUL *smiles in pride that one name is his.* CHRISTIAN *looks forward in much trepidation. The sound of a clamorous fair in the distance, growing closer and louder.*)

*

End of Part One

***

Part Two

10
VANITY FAIR

(*Enter a* BARKER *for the Fair.*)

BARKER: Roll up! Roll up! Ladies and germs. Vanity of vanities! Welcome to the town called Vanity. At our fine town we keep a Fair and its name – that's right – is Vanity Fair. FOR ALL THAT COMETH IS VANITY!

(*Vanity Fair erupts over the stage.* DECEIVERS, CHEATS, GAMERS, PLAYERS, FOOLS, APES, KNAVES *and* ROGUES *and that of every kind set up their stalls.*)

TRADERS: Houses! Lands! Trades! Places! Titles! Countries! Kingdoms! Lusts! Pleasures! Delights! Whores! Bawds! Husbands! Wives! Children! Masters! Servants! Lives! Bodies! Souls! Silver! Gold! Pearls! Stones! Whatnots!

BARKER: Here are to be seen – and all for nothing – murders, thefts, adulteries, all tinged with the rose-red dye of human blood.

(*A* ROGUE *stabs a* FOOL *to death.* FOOL *dies with a hideous scream. For a moment the Fair is silent then a great laugh erupts and trade recommences. Some* APES *drag off the dead* FOOL *and the* ROGUE *goes free and jolly. Enter* CHRISTIANA *with her* SON *and* DAUGHTER.*)

CHRISTIANA: Remember what I said: stay near me. 'Tis easy to get lost in Vanity.

BARKER: French row! Italian row! German row! Britain row! Vanities of every nation sold!!!

CHRISTIANA: Such lovely finery.

(*The* BARKER *comes to* CHRISTIANA.)

BARKER: What be you looking for Missy?

CHRISTIANA: I'd love to buy a little lace. Don't suppose there's any I could afford.

BARKER: If you want money, I know a stall needs a worker.

CHRISTIANA: A God-send that would be. As long as the job is respectable.

BARKER: O certainly!

CHRISTIANA: Children follow me.

(*The* BARKER *sweeps* CHRISTIANA *into the Fair's hubbub. The* CHILDREN *linger and are approached by traders – him by a* ROGUE *and her by a* BAWD.)

ROGUE: You want to be tied to Mummy's apron strings, do ye? I know where's cheap tobacco. Come on lad, follow me.

BAWD: As pretty a thing as thee ye could earn great riches. Come on follow me, mare.

(*The* CHILDREN *are taken off by* TRADERS. *Re-enter the* BARKER.)

BARKER: This Fair is a very great Fair. ALL THAT COMETH IS VANITY!

(*With this,* CHRISTIANA *and her* CHILDREN *are revealed as denizens of Vanity:* CHRISTIANA *is a trader, her* SON *a knave and her* DAUGHTER *a drab.*)

CHRISTIANA: Get your gaudies! Very cheap. Everything must go!

SON: Something for your pipe sir?

DAUGHTER: A good time? Try me!

CHRISTIANA: Sales! Bargains! Cheap deals!

ALL THREE: VANITIES!

(CHRISTIANA *and her family are now a part of the Fair as* CHRISTIAN *and* FAITHFUL *enter. The hubbub stops at the sight of them.*)

ROGUE: I see from that there raiment of yours, you're not from round these parts.

(*The denizens of the Fair concur.*)

FOOL: Ninnies!

KNAVE: Bedlams!

ROGUE: Right outlandish, ain't ye?!

(*A big laugh then the hubbub of the Fair recommences. The* BAWD *approaches* CHRISTIAN *and* FAITHFUL *with her drab,* CHRISTIAN's *daughter.*)

BAWD: Would you care to sample my wares?

CHRISTIAN: Turn my eyes from beholding vanity!

DAUGHTER: Don't he talk odd?

FAITHFUL: Our trade and traffic's in heaven.

BAWD: Ooh hoity-toity!

(*Laughter.* CHRISTIAN *and* FAITHFUL *talk aside as the trade goes on around them.*)

CHRISTIAN: The end of these people is destruction. Their belly is their god and their glory is their shame.

FAITHFUL: We must keep our eyes on the Celestial City.

(*A* DECEIVER *comes to the* PILGRIMS.)

DECEIVER: Come buy, come buy! What will you buy?

CHRISTIAN: We buy the truth, sir.

(*The Fair is suddenly silent.*)

DECEIVER: Ooh! "We buy the truth."

BAWD:	Wager thou think'st of other things.
ROGUE:	Stuck up runts. Give them a proper smiting!

(*Bad feeling begins to rise in the Fair towards the* PILGRIMS.)

TRADERS:	Sue them! Silence them! Cheek! Idiots! Hypocrites! Wallies! Dolts! Christians!

(*A* GREAT ONE *of the Fair turns up to see what the hubbub is.*)

GREAT ONE:	Hello hello hello. What's going on here then?
SON:	These are causing a terrible trouble.

(*The* GREAT ONE *motions and a* ROGUE *and* KNAVE *arrest the* PILGRIMS.)

GREAT ONE:	Hold them fast!

(*To the* PILGRIMS.) From whence do you come? Whither go ye? Why dress thou in unusual garb?

FAITHFUL:	We are pilgrims and strangers in the world going to Jerusalem the heavenly.
GREAT ONE:	Place these in the stocks right away!

(*A great cheer goes up amongst the crowd. The* ROGUE *and* KNAVE *start beating the* PILGRIMS. CHRISTIAN *and* FAITHFUL *are placed in the stocks. The* TRADERS *throw dirt at them so they are besmeared. The* GREAT ONE *falls laughing at what is befalling them.*)

FAITHFUL:	(*To the crowd.*) We do pray for you all.
CHRISTIAN:	Aim for my other cheek – thou hast missed that.
FOOL:	You only had to ask!

(*The* FOOL *bespatters* CHRISTIAN's *other cheek with filth. Laughter. A* CONSIDERATE GENT *of the Fair has been observing their treatment.*)

GENT: These are peaceful and patient fellows. Why this continual abuse? Deservest they such harsh treatment?

(*A small group of Fair dwellers agree.* ROGUE *notices.*)

ROGUE: You in their confederacy?

GENT: They are quiet and sober men.

ROGUE: Perhaps you'd like to join 'em?

GENT: Thou art more worthy of the stocks than they.

ROGUE: Come here and say that!

GENT: I will gladly.

(GENT *goes to* ROGUE *and punches him.*)

ROGUE: Oi!

(*A fight breaks out between those who would abuse the* PILGRIMS *and those who would defend them. The* GREAT ONE *blows his whistle.*)

GREAT ONE: Order, order. Let's have some order!

(*The fighting stops.*)

We shall not have such times at our Fair.

(*He turns to the* PILGRIMS.)

What contentions ye do bring with ye!

(*To his assistants.*) Hang irons 'pon them and lead them about for an example and terror, lest anyone should speak further on their behalf.

(*Irons are hung upon the* PILGRIMS *and they are led up and down.*)

GENT: How they do bear all with patience and meekness! A very great shame on our Fair.

ROGUE: Still thou defendeth them?

GENT: Aye, and will as long as they are abused!

(*This puts the* ROGUE *in even more of a rage and the fighting breaks out again. The* GREAT ONE *blows his whistle again. He turns to the* PILGRIMS.)

GREAT ONE: Neither stocks nor irons will halt such as these. Causing a general riot! Hence with them to gaol. Take 'em away!

(CHRISTIAN *and* FAITHFUL *are led away to gaol.*)

For this abuse they've done they ought to die.

(*The Fair packs away for the night as* CHRISTIAN *and* FAITHFUL *languish in gaol.*)

CHRISTIAN: This calls to my mind the prophecy of our faithful friend Evangelist.

FAITHFUL: One or both of us must suffer the death.

CHRISTIAN: Let us pray.

(*They part a little and pray aside.*)

Lord I am sore afraid. What if I make a bad death and so put my religion to shame? Help me count the grave as my house. To make the bed my darkness. To say to corruption, "Thou art my father," and to the worm, "Thou art my sister and mother."

(*After his prayer* CHRISTIAN *still shivers and shakes.*)

FAITHFUL: My Lord, one of us must run this course the full distance. For the sake of my heart which yearns so for thee, make me the man marked for slaughter. Make my end a perfect imitation of thee.

(*After his prayer,* FAITHFUL *is collected and calm. They turn to each other.*)

We must be content in all conditions to abide.

(CHRISTIAN *half-smiles an unconvincing agreement. Dawn comes.*)

CHRISTIAN: Behold the sun rise.

(*Enter the* GAOLER. *He points to* FAITHFUL.)

GAOLER: You.

(GAOLER *roughly yanks* FAITHFUL *from the cell.* CHRISTIAN *watches him go.*)

CHRISTIAN: I dreamed I'd found a brother to go with me on the way.

Now Vanity wrenches him away from me.

(*The gaol recedes.*)

*

11
THE TRIAL OF FAITHFUL

(CHRISTIAN *observes as a courtroom forms around* FAITHFUL *who stands in the dock.*)

USHER:	All rise for the honourable judge, the Lord Hategood.
	(LORD HATEGOOD *enters the courtroom. He pounds his gavel.*)
HATEGOOD:	Read the indictment.
USHER:	Milord, this man is a disturber of our trade in Vanity. He hath sown divisions and commotions in our town.
	(HATEGOOD *turns to* FAITHFUL.)
HATEGOOD:	How do you plead, sir?
FAITHFUL:	I have only set myself up against that which sets itself up against the Highest.
HATEGOOD:	Humph!
FAITHFUL:	I make no disturbance being a man of peace. People were won to us by beholding our innocence and truth. As to the prince thou talk of, he is Beelzebub, the enemy of our Lord. I defy him and all of his wretched crew.
	(*Commotion in the courtroom.* LORD HATEGOOD *pounds his gavel.*)
HATEGOOD:	Silence in court! Call the witnesses.
USHER:	Envy stand forth.
	(ENVY *stands forth.*)
ENVY:	My Lord I have known this man a long time, and will attest upon my oath before this honourable bench that he –

HATEGOOD: Hold! Give him his oath.

                (*The* USHER *hands* ENVY *the Bible.*)

ENVY: I swear by Almighty God that the evidence I shall give shall be the truth, whole truth, and nothing but the truth, so God help me.

HATEGOOD: Very good. Carry on.

ENVY: My Lord, this man is one of the vilest in our land. He regards not law or convention, people nor prince. I heard him once affirm that the customs of Vanity and Christianity are diametrically opposed. Thus he not only condemns our laudable doings but also us in doing them.

HATEGOOD: Hast thou no more?

ENVY: My Lord I could say much more, only I would not be tedious. Yet if need be when the others have given their evidence – rather than anything be wanted to despatch him – I will enlarge my testimony.

HATEGOOD: Stand by.

                (ENVY *stands by.*)

USHER: Call Superstition.

                (SUPERSTITION *stands forth.*)

HATEGOOD: What can you say for our Prince against him?

SUPERSTITION: My lord, I have no great acquaintance with this man. Nor do I desire any further knowledge of him. But this I know – he is a very pestilent fellow! In some discourse I had the other day with him in this town, I heard him say that our religion was naught and that a man could not please God with it.

                (SUPERSTITION *stands down.*)

HATEGOOD: Very interesting. Next!

USHER:	Call forth Pickthank.

(PICKTHANK *stands forth*.)

PICKTHANK: My lord and you gentlemen all, this fellow I have known a long time and have heard him speak many things that ought not to be spoken. For he hath railed on our noble Prince Beelzebub and contemptibly spoke of his honourable friends such as the Lord Oldman, Lord Carnal Delight, the Lord Luxurious, the Lord Desire of Vainglory, my old Lord Lechery, Sir Having Greedy, with all the rest of our nobility: and he hath moreover said that if all men were of his mind, then these noble men should no longer reside in this town!

(*General consternation at this.*)

Besides, he hath not been afraid to rail on you milord, who are now appointed to be his judge, calling you an ungodly villain with other defaming terms with which he hath bespattered all of the gentry of our town.

HATEGOOD: Stand down.

(LORD HATEGOOD *turns to* FAITHFUL.)

Thou runagate, heretic, and traitor! Hast thou heard what these honest gentlemen have said against thee?

FAITHFUL: May I speak a few words in my own defence?

JUDGE: Sirrah, sirrah! Thou deservest to live no longer, but to be slain immediately on the place. Yet that all men may see our gentleness towards thee, let us hear what vile apostasy has to say.

FAITHFUL: I say then – in answer to what Envy hath spoken – I never said aught but this: that what rule or laws or customs or people were against the word of God are diametrically opposite to Christianity. If I am amiss in this, convince me of my error and I will readily make my recantation.

(LORD HATEGOOD *glowers*.)

As to Superstition, I said only this – That in the worship of God there is required a divine faith, but there can be no divine faith without revelation.

HATEGOOD: Oh, can there not be?

FAITHFUL: To what Mr Pickthank hath to say...

HATEGOOD: Shut him up!!! Gag him!

(FAITHFUL *is gagged*.)

The only voice we wish now to hear is that of the jury.

(*A twelve person* JURY *is revealed in all their horribleness*.)

Ladies and Gents of the jury, you see this man whom hath caused such great uproar in this town. It lieth in your breasts to hang or save him. Let me say this – for the treason he hath confessed, he warrants to die the death. What say you, Mr Blind Man?

BLIND MAN: I clearly see this man is an heretic.

HATEGOOD: Mrs No-Good?

NO-GOOD: Away from the earth with such fellows!

HATEGOOD: Mr Malice?

MALICE: Aye, for I hate the very look of him.

HATEGOOD: Mr Love-Lust?

LOVE-LUST: I never could endure him.

HATEGOOD: Mrs Live-Loose?

LIVE-LOOSE: Nor I, for he is always condemning me.

HATEGOOD: Mr Heady?

HEADY: Hang him! Hang him!

HATEGOOD: Madame High-Mind?

HIGH-MIND: A sorry scrub.

HATEGOOD: Ms Enmity?

ENMITY: My heart riseth against him.

HATEGOOD: Mr Liar?

LIAR: A rogue!

HATEGOOD: Mrs Cruelty?

CRUELTY: Hanging's too good for him.

HATEGOOD: Mr Hate-Light?

HATE-LIGHT: Let us despatch him out of the way.

HATEGOOD: Mr Implacable?

IMPLACABLE: He and I could not be reconciled if I had all the world given to me. Let us bring him in guilty of death.

                (LORD HATEGOOD *places a black cap upon his head and turns to* FAITHFUL.)

HATEGOOD: Sirrah, thou are condemned to be took from this court to the place of the skull, there to be put to the most cruel death imaginable. Take him down!

                (FAITHFUL *is taken from the court.* CHRISTIAN *watches from the prison as his friend is taken to a lonely place and there scourged, buffeted, his flesh lanced with knives, stoned with stones, pricked with swords and lastly burned to ashes at the stake.* CHRISTIAN *hangs his head as the* CROWD *departs, exhausted. The* GAOLER *opens the door.*)

GAOLER: As for you, you're free to go.

                (GAOLER *pushes* CHRISTIAN *out of the gaol onto the road.* CHRISTIAN *stands dejected.*)

CHRISTIAN: I have dreamed such cruelties and horrors! I shall never drive the nightmares from my mind. If that death were too a dream …

FAITHFUL: Brother, above you!

(CHRISTIAN *looks up and has a vision of* FAITHFUL *in a fiery chariot surrounded by* SHINING ONES.)

I am in the City Celestial!
Abundance of Glory is mine.
I am with our Lord.
Exulted I am!

(*The* SHINING ONES *sing.*)

SHINING ONES: Hallelujah!!! Gloria!!!

CHRISTIAN: O, my Faithful brother!

(CHRISTIAN *falls into a swoon. The vision of* FAITHFUL *amidst the* SHINING ONES *disappears.* CHRISTIAN *comes to and sees a fresh-faced young man whose name is* HOPEFUL *bringing him around with a cup of fresh water.*)

HOPEFUL: Friend, my name is Hopeful. I am desirous of leaving this town of Vanity. For too long it hath been my home. I saw your friend die for Truth, and this hath persuaded me to fly to the Celestial City. May I enter into a brotherly covenant and join you?

(CHRISTIAN *rises to* HOPEFUL.)

CHRISTIAN: I am willing to have you with me with all my heart.

(*They embrace.* CHRISTIAN *takes the hand of* HOPEFUL *and they set off together down the road. As they disappear from sight,* CHRISTIANA *is coming out of her own nightmare.*)

CHRISTIANA: What on earth was I dreaming of? Working a thirteen hour day for scarce a shilling!

(*She shouts.*)

Daughter! Son!

(*Her* DAUGHTER *and* SON *appear, the worse for wear.*)

DAUGHTER: Anything important, Mother?

SON: What d'you want?

CHRISTIANA: Don't you give me no lip, child. We're gonna leave old Vanity Town.

(*The* CHILDREN *baulk.*)

No disputing! Follow me.

(*They take her hand and the three of them depart.* MERCY *appears to welcome them home.*)

MERCY: Into the arms of Mercy.

(MERCY *helps them across the threshold of their home.*)

*

12
BY-ENDS

(CHRISTIAN *and* HOPEFUL *walk on hand in hand. They overtake one whose name is* BY-ENDS)

CHRISTIAN: What countryman, sir? And how far go ye?

BY-ENDS: I hail from Fairspeech, gents, and I hence to the Celestial City.

CHRISTIAN: From Fairspeech! Be there any good that live there?

BY-ENDS: I hope so, yes.

CHRISTIAN: What may I call you?

BY-ENDS: I'll be glad of your company if you be going my way. If not, I must be content.

CHRISTIAN: This town of Fairspeech I have heard much of. A wealthy place.

BY-ENDS: I've numerous rich kindred there.

CHRISTIAN: If I may be so bold, who are your kindred?

BY-ENDS: Sir, the whole moneyed town! To tell you true, I myself am become a gentleman of good quality. Yet my great-grandfather was a waterman, looking one way and rowing another. I got my estate the same way.

CHRISTIAN: Are you married?

BY-ENDS: My wife's the spawn of a virtuous woman – she's my Lady Feigning's daughter. 'Tis true we differ somewhat in religion from those of the stricter sort on two small points. We never strive against wind and tide, and we are always most zealous when religion goes in his silver slippers. We love much to walk with him in the street when people applaud it.

(CHRISTIAN *holds* HOPEFUL *back, allowing* BY-ENDS *to walk a little ahead.*)

CHRISTIAN: It runs in my mind that this is one By-Ends of Fairspeech. If it be he, we have in our company a very great knave.

HOPEFUL: Ask him. Methinks he'll not be ashamed of his name.

(CHRISTIAN *walks to* BY-ENDS.)

CHRISTIAN: Sir, is not your name Mr By-Ends of Fairspeech?

BY-ENDS: That is not my name! It is a nickname given to me by them as can't abide me. I must be content to put up with it.

CHRISTIAN: You never gave men occasion to name you thus?

BY-ENDS: Never! The worst I ever did was that I've had the luck to jump in my judgement with the present way of the times – whatever it was – and my chance was thereby to gain.

CHRISTIAN: The name suits you better than you're willing to say.

BY-ENDS: If you imagine thus, I cannot help it.

CHRISTIAN: If you do go with us you must go against wind and tide. You must also own religion in his rags as well as his silver slippers, and stand by him too when bound in irons as well as in the streets with applause.

BY-ENDS: You mustn't impose it over my faith. Leave me my liberty and let me go with you.

CHRISTIAN: Not a step further unless you do as we say.

BY-ENDS: I shall not desert my old principles. They are harmless and profitable. If I may not go with you, I'll do as I did before – go by myself until someone comes that will be glad of me.

CHRISTIAN: Good riddance to you, sir.

(CHRISTIAN *motions for* HOPEFUL *to hurry and the two go a distance ahead of* BY-ENDS. BY-ENDS *is now joined by three fellows*: MR HOLD-THE-WORLD, MR MONEY-LOVE *and* MR SAVE-ALL.)

HOLD-THE-WORLD: By the Devil! If it isn't our old friend Mr By-Ends. How are you?

BY-ENDS: Mr Hold-the-World! Fancy meeting you here. My good companions Money-Love and Save-All. It's long time indeed since us four were convoked.

SAVE-ALL: That it is, that it is. Not since our minority as schoolfellows. Each well taught by Mr Gripeman of that dear little market town Love-Gain in the county of Coveting.

MONEY-LOVE: What pains he took to teach us the good arts of getting by violence, fraud, flattery, lying, or putting on religion's guise. Methinks we all gained so much from our master we could open a school of getting, each of us!

(*The four men chuckle.*)

SAVE-ALL: Who are they on the road before us?

BY-ENDS: They are a pair of fair countrymen that after their mode are going on pilgrimage.

MONEY-LOVE: Why did they not stay, that we might have had their good company?

BY-ENDS: Beshrew them! Those men are so rigid that even if a man be never so godly, if he jumps not with them in all things, they thrust him out of their troupe.

SAVE-ALL: Men over-righteous.

BY-ENDS: They are for hazarding all for God. As you know, I am for taking any advantage to secure my estate and my life.

HOLD-THE-WORLD: For my part I count him as but a fool that having the liberty to keep what he has shall be so imprudent as to lose it. Let us be wise as serpents. Abraham and Solomon grew rich in religion. Job says that "a good man shall lay up gold as dust."

SAVE-ALL: I think we're all agreed in this matter.

HOLD-THE-WORLD: Aye we are.

(*All agree.*)

My brethren give me leave to propound a question to these gentlemen, seeing as they so strongly opposed our good friend Mr By-Ends.

BY-ENDS: You shall see the foolishness of their arguments.

(HOLD-THE-WORLD *calls to* CHRISTIAN *and* HOPEFUL.)

HOLD-THE-WORLD: Sirs!

CHRISTIAN: What would you?

HOLD-THE-WORLD: We should like to propound a short question to you of religion.

CHRISTIAN: I shall oblige.

HOLD-THE-WORLD: Suppose a man – a minister or a tradesman – should have an advantage lie before him to get life's good blessings. Yet he can by no means come by them except – in appearance at least – he becomes extraordinarily zealous in some point of religion what he'd not meddled with before. May not he use this means to attain his better end, and yet be considered a right honest fellow?

CHRISTIAN: We know it be unlawful to follow Christ for loaves.

HOPEFUL: For John, chapter six clearly states so.

CHRISTIAN: (*To* HOPEFUL.) Many thanks.

(*To the others*) So how much more abominable is it to make Him and religion a stalking horse to get hold of and enjoy the world! Nor do we find any of this opinion other than heathens, hypocrites, witches, and, aye, Satans. For Judas the devil was religious for the bag that he might be possessed of the wealth therein.

(HOLD-THE-WORLD *and his companions shrink somewhat at this.*)

The man that takes up religion for the world will throw it away for the same. Judas sold religion and his Master for it. Your rewards are according to your works.

HOPEFUL: Such is sound.

(BY-ENDS *and his company squirm.*)

BY-ENDS: We'll tarry a short while here. You're surely keen to be off on your journey. Fare thee well.

CHRISTIAN: Think on't.

(*To* HOPEFUL.) Come.

(CHRISTIAN *and* HOPEFUL *carry forwards upon their journey as* BY-ENDS *and the rest shrink backwards into the outer darkness.*)

What shall these say when rebuked not by mortal men but by the devouring conflagration.

(CHRISTIAN *stomps onwards.* HOPEFUL *hurries after him.*)

*

13
GIANT DESPAIR

(The way becomes rough and discouraging. They pass by a meadow, and a stile to go over into it. A sign on the stile reads "By-Path Meadow". CHRISTIAN goes over to the stile and looks into the meadow.)

CHRISTIAN: Here is easier going. Come, good Hopeful.

HOPEFUL: What if this path should lead us out of the way?

CHRISTIAN: It goes by our edge!

(HOPEFUL is uneasy.)

HOPEFUL: Oh alright. You persuade me...

(CHRISTIAN and HOPEFUL climb over the stile and enter By-Path meadow.)

CHRISTIAN: How much easier on our foot soles be this.

(CHRISTIAN and HOPEFUL go further in the meadow. It begins to grow dark. A little way off they hear a cry as if one falls down a pit.)

HOPEFUL: What was that?

CHRISTIAN: I'm not sure. But I know what it sounded like.

HOPEFUL: What?

CHRISTIAN: A man named Vain-Confidence falling into a pit.

(It has grown very dark. A bad storm begins.)

HOPEFUL: O that I had kept on my way!

CHRISTIAN: Who would have thought this path should lead us out of it?

HOPEFUL: I was afraid of it from the first and gave you that little caution. I would have spoken plainer but you are older than me.

CHRISTIAN: I am sorry to have put thee in danger. I had no evil intent. Pray brother, forgive me.

HOPEFUL: I do forgive thee, and also believe that this shall be for our benefit.

(*Storm all the more. The* PILGRIMS *are hopelessly lost and travel in circles in darkness. Eventually they see a castle gate.*)

CHRISTIAN: What is that ahead of us?

HOPEFUL: Looks like a castle.

CHRISTIAN: Let us seek shelter there.

(*The* PILGRIMS *hurry to and through the gate. They find themselves in a barren stone courtyard.*)

This courtyard shall be dry for the night, and the storm will be gone by the morning.

(CHRISTIAN *and* HOPEFUL *huddle down in the courtyard and sleep. The day breaks.* CHRISTIAN *wakes up, bleary-eyed and heavy. He nudges his companion.*)

Shall we go?

HOPEFUL: Let's go.

(*They do not move. The shadow of a colossus comes over them: this is* GIANT DESPAIR.)

CHRISTIAN: The name of this Castle is surely Doubting.

HOPEFUL: Its guardian must be that giant named Despair.

(*A door is slammed shut.* CHRISTIAN *and* HOPEFUL *lie on the floor apart, unable to move.*)

HOPEFUL: Really very nasty.

CHRISTIAN: To my spirit it stinks.

HOPEFUL: Not a bite to drink nor drop of bread.

CHRISTIAN: Nil luminosity.

HOPEFUL: No one ever bothers to ask, "how you doing?"

CHRISTIAN: No contacts nor any acquaintances.

HOPEFUL: A clog on the leg of a bird to hinder her flight.

(*They hang their heads in the dungeon.*)

CHRISTIAN: I brought us to this plight!

(CHRISTIAN *beats himself up.* HOPEFUL *stares into the distance.*)

HOPEFUL: I never gave thee a word of distaste but thou hates me.

(HOPEFUL *ignores his friend's actions, rolls up his own sleeve and tries to cut himself with a broken shard.*)

Woe is I.

CHRISTIAN: Abaddon-ed.

(*They self-harm in sighs and lamentations then* CHRISTIAN *turns on* HOPEFUL.)

HOPEFUL: A halter. Poison. A knife.

CHRISTIAN: Why choose life?

HOPEFUL: Please let me go!

CHRISTIAN: We can never go.

(*The* PILGRIMS *have terrible fits then calm a little.*)

Brother what shall we? This existence we now live is misery. My soul chooses strangling rather than life.

HOPEFUL: Death would be more welcome than forever thus to abide. But our Lord hath forbid us suicide. Talkest of ease in the grave? Hast thou forgotten hell? Others have been in the hands of this Giant Despair and escaped. Let us endure awhile and wait patiently.

CHRISTIAN: Thou hast a little jot restrained my mind.

(*But* CHRISTIAN *again changes his mind.*)

          O let us do away with thee and I!

HOPEFUL: Brother remember now thy past valiance. Apollyon nor the Valley of the Shadow of Death could crush thee. Thou seest I am with thee in this dungeon – a far weaker man than thou. The Giant has also wounded me and cut off the bread from my mouth. I mourn with thee sans the light but let us exercise endurance. Bear up best as we can.

CHRISTIAN: The return of night.

          (CHRISTIAN *and* HOPEFUL *sink down again.*)

          A lamentable case all Saturday. As ever. As before.

HOPEFUL: Brother let us pray all the more.

          (CHRISTIAN *unenthusiastically agrees. The* PILGRIMS *pray. As they do, a little chink of light breaks into the dungeon.* CHRISTIAN *looks up as one half amazed.*)

CHRISTIAN: What a fool am I thus in a stinking dungeon to lie when I may as well walk out at liberty! I've in my bosom a key called Promise that will open all locks in this Castle of Doubt.

HOPEFUL: Good news my brother. Pluck it out of thy bosom and try!

          (CHRISTIAN *pulls the key out of his bosom and tries the dungeon door. The bolt gives back.*)

CHRISTIAN: It works fine!

          (*Light floods in as the two* PILGRIMS *are back at the stile, again standing in the way. They hug in relief and set off again.*)

                  *

14

THE SHEPHERDS OF THE DELECTABLE MOUNTAINS

(*The* PILGRIMS *climb, soon rising to the Delectable Mountains. Four shepherds* – KNOWLEDGE, EXPERIENCE, WATCHFUL *and* SINCERE – *are there.* CHRISTIAN *approaches* KNOWLEDGE.)

CHRISTIAN: Whose Delectable Mountains are these?

KNOWLEDGE: These be Immanuel's land.

CHRISTIAN: And whose be the sheep that feed on them?

KNOWLEDGE: The sheep are He's.

HOPEFUL: How far is the Celestial City from here?

KNOWLEDGE: Too far for any but those that arrive.

HOPEFUL: Is there any relief in this place for weary pilgrims?

SINCERE: We never neglect to entertain strangers.

(*The* SHEPHERDS *take the* PILGRIMS *into their tents to warm and feed them. As this happens, the* SHEPHERDS *play their pipes and sing "The Lamb" by William Blake.*)

SHEPHERDS: Little Lamb who made thee?
Dost thou know who made thee?
Gave thee life & bid thee feed
By the stream & o'er the mead.
Gave thee clothing of delight
Softest clothing woolly bright.
Gave thee such a tender voice
Making all the vales rejoice!
Little Lamb who made thee?
Dost thou know who made thee?

(*This done,* KNOWLEDGE *speaks.*)

KNOWLEDGE: Shall we show these pilgrims wonders?

HOPEFUL: O do please!

(*The* SHEPHERDS *laugh and lead the* PILGRIMS *forth up into the Mountains.*)

KNOWLEDGE: Glance ye down. This first peak be called Error.

(*The* PILGRIMS *look down and recoil.*)

CHRISTIAN: What meaneth this?

KNOWLEDGE: Those dashed in pieces at floor are them clambered up too high.

EXPERIENCE: To Caution peak.

(*They ascend another peak.* EXPERIENCE *points down.*)

The men stumbling 'mongst the yonder tomb are blind.

CHRISTIAN: This meaneth?

EXPERIENCE: They were captured and thrown into Doubting Castle by Giant Despair who put out their eyes: "He that wanders out of the way of understanding shall remain in the congregation of the dead."

(*The* SHEPHERDS *begin to leave this peak but* CHRISTIAN *and* HOPEFUL *look down then at each other, tears gushing from their eyes.*)

WATCHFUL: Come! The next peak.

(*The* SHEPHERDS *and* PILGRIMS *ascend the next peak. As they look down, there is a rumbling sound as of fire.*)

CHRISTIAN: What meaneth this? All's dark and smoky.

WATCHFUL: This is the byway to hell. A way hypocrites go in at. Such as sell their birthright with Esau, or with Judas sell their Lord.

HOPEFUL: I perceive that these had on them, every one, a show of pilgrimage.

WATCHFUL: Yes, and held it a long time.

(*By now both* CHRISTIAN *and* HOPEFUL *are shaking from the sights they have seen.*)

SINCERE: Let us next show with our perspective glass the City Celestial's gates.

(*The other* SHEPHERDS *agree and the* PILGRIMS *ascend another peak.* SINCERE *produces two perspective glasses.*)

This peak is the hill called Clear. Look through here.

(SINCERE *gives the* PILGRIMS *the glasses but their hands shake so much that they can barely look through them.*)

CHRISTIAN: I see something like the gate!

HOPEFUL: See a little of the glory of the place!

(SINCERE *retrieves the glasses.*)

SINCERE: Thou shalt see it all face to face.

(*The* PILGRIMS *and the* SHEPHERDS *descend the Mountains as the* SHEPHERDS *pipe and sing.*)

SHEPHERDS: Thus by the shepherds secrets are revealed
Which from all other men are kept concealed.
Come to the shepherds then if you would see
Things deep things hid and that mysterious be.

(*The* PILGRIMS *are back at the wayside.*)

KNOWLEDGE: Here be a note of the way.

EXPERIENCE: Beware the Flatterer.

WATCHFUL: Take heed to sleep ye not on Enchanted Ground.

SINCERE: God speed.

(*The* SHEPHERDS *pipe the* PILGRIMS *on their way.*)

*

15

IGNORANCE, THE FLATTERER, ATHEIST, AND THE ENCHANTED GROUND

(As CHRISTIAN and HOPEFUL go on, a very brisk lad comes by them; his name is IGNORANCE.)

CHRISTIAN: Who art thou neighbour, and where art thou going?

IGNORANCE: My name is Ignorance. I head for the City Celestial.

CHRISTIAN: Thou mayest have some difficulty getting in the gate.

IGNORANCE: I've led a good life.

CHRISTIAN: However you think of yourself, you'll not be allowed in.

IGNORANCE: I hope all will be well.

CHRISTIAN: You're wise in your own conceit.

(Aside to HOPEFUL.) There's more hope of a fool than of him. Let's outgo him at present then stop for him again, see if we can correct him by degrees.

(CHRISTIAN and HOPEFUL agree and hurry on. IGNORANCE watches them go.)

IGNORANCE: Well go thou. I, Ignorance, follow thee.

(IGNORANCE follows them down the road.)

CHRISTIAN: May God deliver us from the next uncircumcised Philistine we meet.

(They come to a crossroads.)

HOPEFUL: The road forks.

CHRISTIAN: One way seems as straight as the other.

HOPEFUL: Surely this is our way?

CHRISTIAN: I wish I could be certain brother.

(The FLATTERER enters in a robe of white.)

FLATTERER: Why dost thou stand so forlorn?

CHRISTIAN: We're wondering which is the way to the City Celestial.

FLATTERER: I go hither. Follow me. You two are precisely the breed of most excellent and virtuous pilgrims I wish to have with me on the way.

(*The* PILGRIMS *begin to follow the* FLATTERER. *By degrees the road he leads them down turns and turns. By and by, before they are aware, he leads them within the compass of a net, in which they both get so entangled that they know not what to do. The* FLATTERER *smiles and leaves them lamenting.*)

CHRISTIAN: Did the Shepherds not bid us beware of the Flatterer?

HOPEFUL: We also forgot to read their note of directions about the way.

CHRISTIAN: Now are we lost in destroyer's trails.

(*A* SHINING ONE *appears carrying a whip.*)

SHINING ONE: Who art thou?

CHRISTIAN: Poor pilgrims were bound for Zion.

SHINING ONE: Why here?

HOPEFUL: We followed a man dressed in white.

(*The* SHINING ONE *sighs and untangles them from the net.*)

SHINING ONE: A Flatterer! A false apostle that hath disguised himself as an angel of light.

(*The* SHINING ONE *has rent the net and they are free.*)

Lay down. "A wicked man is worthy to be beat."

(*The* PILGRIMS *reluctantly do so. The* SHINING ONE *whips them.*

As this happens, CHRISTIANA *is back at home, giving her confession to* MERCY.)

CHRISTIANA: I mocked my husband when he held forth that we dwell in the City of Destruction. I caused him to go off on his pilgrimage alone. I've dragged myself and my darlings to the brink of annihilation. I expect due punishment to be mine.

MERCY: Was not almost coming to loss enough of itself to rebuke thee? Go thyself that way to where the friend to sinners is King.

(CHRISTIANA *and* MERCY *take leave to consider this. The* SHINING ONE *has finished whipping the* PILGRIMS.)

SHINING ONE: All them that He loves, He reproves and disciplines.

(*The* SHINING ONE *departs.* CHRISTIAN *and* HOPEFUL *rise and continue their journey in silence. They spot one coming to meet them.*)

CHRISTIAN: Yonder comes a man to meet us with back toward Zion.

HOPEFUL: Let us take heed, lest he too be a Flatterer.

(ATHEIST *enters to them.*)

ATHEIST: Where are you travelling?

CHRISTIAN: Mount Zion.

(ATHEIST *falls to very great laughter.*)

Why do you laugh?

ATHEIST: What ignorant persons you are! Taking upon you so tedious a journey, yet you are like to have nothing for your pains but the trouble of the road.

CHRISTIAN: You do not think we'll be received at the City?

ATHEIST: Received? In all this world there is no such place as this city of which you dream.

CHRISTIAN: In the world to come...

ATHEIST: When I was back home, I heard as you assert and went to find this city. I have been seeking it for twenty years but have found nothing.

HOPEFUL: We both believe there is such a place.

ATHEIST: Had I not at home believed, I should not have come this distance. Finding nothing, I go back home, and will seek for myself afresh those things which, for hopes non-existent, I cast away.

(CHRISTIAN *and* HOPEFUL *speak aside.*)

CHRISTIAN: Could it be true what he sayeth?

HOPEFUL: We saw Mount Zion from the Delectable Mountains. Let's cease to hear him to save our souls.

CHRISTIAN: I asked to test you.

HOPEFUL: Did you?

CHRISTIAN: Safe in the truth of our beliefs, let us leave.

(*The* PILGRIMS *press on,* ATHEIST *laughing at them as they go. His laughter resounds, multiplies, until at last it seems that the whole world is laughing at* CHRISTIAN *and* HOPEFUL. *Now they enter into the Enchanted Ground as the laughter fades. The two* PILGRIMS *grow drowsy as they walk.*)

HOPEFUL: Let us lie down here and nap.

CHRISTIAN: By no means, lest we never more awake.

HOPEFUL: Sleep is sweet to the worker.

CHRISTIAN: The shepherds bid us beware of Enchanted Ground.

HOPEFUL: I see it is true that "two are better than one."

(IGNORANCE *appears behind them.*)

Look how yonder youngster still loiters. Let us try him again.

CHRISTIAN: (*Calling to* IGNORANCE.) Come away man. Why stay you behind?

IGNORANCE: I take my pleasure in walking alone.

CHRISTIAN: Come up. Let us talk away the time.

(IGNORANCE *reluctantly catches them up as they wait for him.*)

How stands it now betwixt God and thy soul?

IGNORANCE: Well, I hope. I am always full of good notions.

CHRISTIAN: What good notions?

IGNORANCE: I think a lot of heaven and God.

CHRISTIAN: So do the devils and the damned.

IGNORANCE: I think of them and desire them.

CHRISTIAN: The soul of the sluggard desires and has not.

IGNORANCE: I think of them and leave all for them.

CHRISTIAN: Why dost thou think thou hast done that?

IGNORANCE: My heart informs me.

CHRISTIAN: "He that trusts his own heart is a fool."

IGNORANCE: Mine is a good heart.

CHRISTIAN: Prove it.

IGNORANCE: It comforts me with heavenly hopes.

CHRISTIAN: That may be its deceitfulness.

IGNORANCE: My heart and my life agree.

CHRISTIAN: Who told thee so?

IGNORANCE: My heart tells me.

CHRISTIAN: "Ask my fellow if I be a thief!"

IGNORANCE: Does not a good heart have good thoughts?

CHRISTIAN: It's one thing to have good thoughts but another to only think so.

IGNORANCE: I'll never believe my heart is bad!

CHRISTIAN: Thou never had one good thought in thy life. The Word of God says crooked and perverse are man's ways. None know themselves as God knows them.

IGNORANCE: You think me such a fool as to think that I can see further than God?

CHRISTIAN: How dost thou think in this matter?

IGNORANCE: I believe in Christ. He'll justify me.

CHRISTIAN: Why believe in Christ seeing as thou hast no need for him?! Thou seest not thy infirmities. Thou hast such a high opinion of thyself as renders thee one that never saw need for Christ to justify thee. How can you say, "I believe in Him?"

IGNORANCE: I believe well enough for all that.

CHRISTIAN: True faith flies the soul to Christ for a refuge. Under His skirt the soul is shrouded, then presented as spotless to God. Only then is it accepted and acquitted.

IGNORANCE: Would you have us trust to what Christ do whether we be good or ill? This conceit loosens the reins of our lusts!

CHRISTIAN: Ignorance is thy name. As thy name is so art thou.

HOPEFUL: Ask him if he ever had Christ revealed to him from heaven.

IGNORANCE: Are ye men for revelations?! They are the fruits of distracted brains.

HOPEFUL: Christ cannot be known but by revelations.

CHRISTIAN: Such knowledge thou art ignorant of. Poor Ignorance.

(IGNORANCE *halts*.)

IGNORANCE: I cannot keep pace with you. Go. I'll stay behind.

(CHRISTIAN *and* HOPEFUL *halt and look upon* IGNORANCE.)

CHRISTIAN: Good counsel saves, if well taken.

(*To* HOPEFUL.) Come good Hopeful. We must walk by ourselves again.

(CHRISTIAN *and* HOPEFUL *shake the dust from their shoes and hurry on, leaving* IGNORANCE *to hobble behind them.*)

Pities me much for this poor man. 'Twill go ill for him at the last.

HOPEFUL: Our place is still the Enchanted Land, and my eyes still long to droop.

CHRISTIAN: Shall we fall on some profitable question?

HOPEFUL: Aye.

CHRISTIAN: Let's meditate on backsliding.

HOPEFUL: We could...

CHRISTIAN: There are in my judgement nine stages to backsliding.

HOPEFUL: Nine?

CHRISTIAN: Yes nine. First, men draw their thoughts away from the remembrance of God. The second one...

(*They walk ever on,* CHRISTIAN *gesticulating and lecturing – us hearing only numbers and the odd harsh word such as "guilt" or "damned" or "sinner" – until he reaches the end of his sermon.*)

...until ninthly their hearts are hard as adamantine and they everlastingly perish in their own deceivings, unless a miracle of grace occur.

*

16
BEULAH & THE RIVER OF DEATH

(HOPEFUL *gasps.*)

CHRISTIAN: What?

HOPEFUL: You feel it?

CHRISTIAN: What?

HOPEFUL: I have a feeling we're not on Enchanted Ground anymore.

CHRISTIAN: The air's very sweet and pleasant.

HOPEFUL: As the bridegroom over his bride, God rejoices over us!

(*Melodious music surrounds them as* FOUR SHINING ONES *walk forth singing.*)

SHINING ONES: Rise up my love, my fair one come away.
For winter is now past, the rain is gone.
Flowers on the earth.
The singing of the birds.
And the voice of the turtle dove is heard.

(*The* SHINING ONES *give the* PILGRIMS *bread and wine.*)

CHRISTIAN: All my life I've felt forsaken. Walking desolate down the way. Now my willing mind is full of joy!

HOPEFUL: I feel as if I am married to all that surrounds.

(CHRISTIAN *collapses into an ecstasy.*)

HOPEFUL: What ails thee, good brother?

CHRISTIAN: If you see my beloved, tell Him I'm sick of love!

HOPEFUL: That makes us twain!

(HOPEFUL *swoons as well and the* PILGRIMS *moan and squirm upon the ground, sick with desire. The* SHINING ONES *watch them. The pangs of love-*

sickness abate a little and the PILGRIMS look up at the SHINING ONES, *a trifle embarrassed.*)

CHRISTIAN: Wherefore do we utter such groanings as cannot be uttered?

SHINING ONE: The wine of these vineyards is so sweet, it causes the lips to be moved so to speak.

(CHRISTIAN *rises, followed by* HOPEFUL.)

CHRISTIAN: I perceive the Celestial City shining ahead of me.

(CHRISTIAN, HOPEFUL *and the* SHINING ONES *are for a moment drenched in a dazzling golden light. All goes dull. A dark river flows before the* PILGRIMS' *feet.*)

SHINING ONE: First must you cross the river to get to the gate.

(CHRISTIAN *and* HOPEFUL *tremble.*)

CHRISTIAN: It looks very deep.

HOPEFUL: Is there no other way?

SHINING ONE: You must go through it.

CHRISTIAN: Are these waters all of a depth?

SHINING ONE: They be as shallow or deep as you believe.

(CHRISTIAN *nods.*)

HOPEFUL: So brother, let's wade in.

CHRISTIAN: Whatever must be done, must be.

(*A gloomy bell begins to toll. The* PILGRIMS *hold hands and wade into the waters. The* SHINING ONES *disappear. The* PILGRIMS *are soon up to their necks and* CHRISTIAN *is in trouble.*)

I sink in deep waters! The billows go over my head!

HOPEFUL: Be of good cheer my brother. I feel the bottom. It's good.

CHRISTIAN: The sorrows of death are about me. I'll not see the land of milk and honey.

(CHRISTIAN *gasps as a great darkness and horror fall over him and he loses grip on* HOPEFUL's *hand.. The* PILGRIMS *drift apart.*)

My senses fail. My sins and my backslidings weigh heavily. What's God want with one such as me?

HOPEFUL: Brother, where art thou?

(CHRISTIAN *begins to go under.*)

CHRISTIAN: Fooled by the Worldly Wiseman!
Slept and lost my Eternal Identity!
I should have died at the Fair for Faithful.
I brought us to Giant Despair.

HOPEFUL: (*Distant.*) Brother!

CHRISTIAN: The very chief of sinners! In all the world there's none worse than I!

(CHRISTIAN *is drowning. Of a sudden* HOPEFUL *reappears.*)

HOPEFUL: Brother, believe! Keep thy head above water. Men stand on the shore to take us to the Gate.

CHRISTIAN: It is for you that they wait. You've been Hopeful since we met.

HOPEFUL: So have you.

CHRISTIAN: Surely if that was correct, He would arise now to help me. For all my sins He's damned me. Brought me to a terrible snare.

(CHRISTIAN *splutters, going down.*)

HOPEFUL: Christian my brother be of good cheer. Jesus Christ makes thee whole truly. Thy sins are all forgiven thee!

(CHRISTIAN *gropes then a light hits him.*)

CHRISTIAN: I see my Lord again! This river shall not overflow me.

(CHRISTIAN *stands, no longer drowning.*)

*

17
THE CELESTIAL CITY

(CHRISTIAN *emerges from the river with* HOPEFUL, *being greeted by two* SHINING ONES.)

SHINING ONES: Thou art very near the City. Walk this way.

> (*The* SHINING ONES *fly forwards, their feet barely touching the ground as they lead* CHRISTIAN *and* HOPEFUL *forwards.*)

HOPEFUL: Brother Christian note how we walk with such ease.

CHRISTIAN: That 'cos we've left our mortal garments in the stream. Everything which dragged us down –

HOPEFUL: All that stuff which stopped our speed –

CHRISTIAN: Former things hath fully passed away.

> (CHRISTIAN *and* HOPEFUL *laugh in bliss then* HOPEFUL *addresses The* SHINING ONES.)

HOPEFUL: Tell us friends about the place.

SHINING ONES: Glory inexpressible! Mount Zion and Jerusalem the Heavenly are there, full of perfected spirits and the angelic company. Now go ye to the Paradise of God wherein thou shalt see the Tree of Life, and eat of its fruits which are never fading. Ye shall have white robes given thee, and you will walk and talk every hour with the King. All the days of Eternity.

CHRISTIAN: What do we in the Holy City?

SHINING ONES: Reap what you've sown – the fruit of all your prayers, tears and sufferings. Wear on your heads crowns of gold. Have perpetual visions of He that is Holy. Attend Him with continual shouting and thanksgiving. Your ears be delighted with seeing. Your eyes with hearing the pleasant voice. When he sits on the throne of judgement you shall have voice in that decree and victory over thy enemies. Behold, the gates of the City are before thee!

(*The* SHINING ONES *and the* PILGRIMS *have reached the Gates of the City. The Gates open and a large company of the* HEAVENLY HOST *come out to greet the* PILGRIMS.)

HOST: Who are these?

SHINING ONES: They who have loved our Lord while in the world. Left all for His holy name. We have brought them from the river.

HOST: Blessed are they that receive an invitation to the marriage of the Lamb!

(*Trumpets sound. The* HOST *rush towards the* PILGRIMS *hugging them and spinning them around.* CHRISTIAN *and* HOPEFUL *cry with joy.*)

CHRISTIAN: No tongue nor pen could ever express this glory-joyous feeling!

(*The* HOST *put them down.*)

HOST: Hast thou thy certificates?

CHRISTIAN: I have.

HOPEFUL: Most positively.

(CHRISTIAN *and* HOPEFUL *present their certificates.*)

HOST: The King must peruse these.

CHRISTIAN: Are we to see the King?!

(*The entire* HOST *turns towards the Gates. They open and the* KING *appears. The* HOST *hands the* PILGRIMS' *certificates to the* KING. *He inspects them, and smiles.*)

KING: Where are these men?

HOST: Without the gate.

KING: The righteous nation which keeps the Truth may enter in.

HOST: (*A great cry.*) HALLELUJAH! GLORIA!

(*The* PILGRIMS *are hoisted upon the shoulders of the* HOST *and carried into the city.*)

BLESSINGS HONOUR AND GLORY
BE FOREVER TO THE LAMB
HOLY! HOLY! HOLY!
IS THE LORD ON HIGH!

(*The* HOST *and the* PILGRIMS *pass through the Gates into the city. The Gates shut behind them. The* TWO SHINING ONES *wait by the Gates.*)

*

18
THE END OF IGNORANCE

(*The* TWO SHINING ONES *stand before the Gates with the* DREAMER *watching. Suddenly* IGNORANCE *runs on.*)

IGNORANCE: What ho, everybody! Ignorance is here.

(*He rushes to the Gates and bangs upon them.*)

Come on. Let me in, somebody!

(*The* SHINING ONES *approach him.*)

SHINING ONES: Whence came you, and what would you have here?

IGNORANCE: I have ate and drank in presence of the King. In the streets I've heard his teaching.

SHINING ONES: Thy certificate?

IGNORANCE: What certificate?

SHINING ONES: We've got a right one here.

(*The* SHINING ONES *laugh grimly and eyeball* IGNORANCE. *He becomes agitated. They stalk around him and he begins to back away. Suddenly they shed their shining garments. They appear as* DEMONS *before him.*)

DEMONS: Hence ye forth from here!

(IGNORANCE *shrieks as The* DEMONS *rush for him. They grab him.*)

IGNORANCE: Some mistake surely?

DEMONS: No mistaking thou for what thou art!

(*The* DEMONS *bind him hand and foot and drag him away from the Gates. They open a trapdoor from which smoke bellows out. The heads of more horrible* DEMONS *bob up from below.* IGNORANCE *struggles and screams. The* DEMONS *swing* IGNORANCE *over the pit.*)

One! Two! Three!!!

(*They throw* IGNORANCE *down into the pit. His screams sound as he falls a long way then fade. One* DEMON *speaks to the other.*)

A DEMON: There is a way to hell even from the gate of Heaven.

(*They slam shut the trap door of the pit.*)

*

19
AWAKENING

(*The* DREAMER *awakes in his bedroom.*)

DREAMER: I awake and behold it was a dream!

(*The* DREAMER's LADY *also awakes in fear.*)

LADY: Mercy! MERCY!

(*The* DREAMER *grabs her.*)

DREAMER: What is it?

(*She stops panicking.*)

LADY: A scary dream.

DREAMER: What did you dream?

LADY: You went and left me, and were accepted into the Heavenly company. I was kept out and many besides me.

DREAMER: That is how my dream comes to an end.

LADY: I believe I must try sleep again and dream a pilgrim dream for me. In my dream I shall not travel alone. I'll take Mercy with me. And my entire family. And a whole community of weak and fearing. A Great Heart will guide and protect us.

DREAMER: You do not like my dream?

LADY: We have different dreams.

(*The* DREAMER *sulks a little.*)

It is your dream has inspired me.

(*She starts to sing.*)

Who would true valour see
Let him come hither.
One here will constant be
Come wind come weather.
There's no discouragement

Shall make him once relent
His first avowed intent
To be a pilgrim.

(*The* DREAMER *joins in.*)

DREAMER & LADY: Who so beset him round
With dismal stories
Do but themselves confound
His strength the more is.
No lion can him fright
He'll with a giant fight
But he will have a right
To be a pilgrim.

(*The entire company appears and joins in.*)

ALL: Hobgoblin nor foul fiend
Can daunt his spirit
He knows he at the end
Shall life inherit.
Then fancies fly away!
He'll fear not what men say
He'll labour night and day
To be a pilgrim.

THE END

***

www.ingramcontent.com/pod-product-compliance
Lightning Source LLC
Chambersburg PA
CBHW051515260626
47162CB00008B/2973